Catch Rider

PREQUEL: STONEGATE SERIES

TUDOR ROBINS

1st edition, 2024 – ISBN 978-1-990802-57-7 (ebook) | ISBN 978-1-990802-58-4 (paperback) | ISBN 978-1-990802-59-1 (audiobook)

Contents

A gift for you!

To receive a free ebook, all you have to do is sign up for my newsletter. It's the only way to get your copy of Hide & Seek. Visit: www.tudorrobins.com/contact, or use this QR code:

By signing up you'll be the first to know about new releases, and to learn about deals on my books and other books you might enjoy.

I hope to see you on the list!

Chapter One

THE RUBBER SOLES OF my running shoes, cold-stiffened, slap the pavement. My breath plumes clouds into the dark morning air. I settle my reflective-trimmed toque more firmly over my ears and welcome the extra strip of warmth it provides.

My core is toasty – on fire. Working. Pumping. But my extremities take a hit in the chill. Especially this time of year, when the cold is new, the frost is fresh, the tinkle of ice at the edge of a puddle a reminder that this is the coldest morning we've had so far. That the temperature's only going one direction from here.

I'll get used to it. Just being out here this morning is a step in that direction. Toughening me for the frigid months to come. Increasing my cardio so I can hop off one horse and onto another, then another, then another all day long – as long as people will give me horses to ride. Strengthening my muscles so I can hold my balance over any fence, staying out of my horse's way. Letting him do the work he needs to clear the jump without me getting in the way.

Which is why, when I reach the end of my street, even as a gust of wind dashes icy pellets against my exposed skin, I mentally check my lungs – there's breath left there, and my muscles – they're nowhere near burning, and I run right on past, into the loop that will give me an extra two kilometres.

And I pick up my pace.

***

The sun's up by the time I give Gri-gri's battle-notched ears a quick good-bye scratch, shoulder my backpack, and deadbolt the front door behind me. The scars on his body are the only tells that the dog – named for his grey coat ("gris" in Spanish) – used to live on the streets in Peru. When my parents brought him home from their first archeological trip ten years ago, he immediately chose a spot for himself on our sofa, adjusting instantly to the cushiness of indoor North American life. He'll sleep in a sunbeam the whole time I'm at school and I'll have to coax him out for his lunchtime walk.

Two years ago, the first time my parents left on a research secondment during the school year, my guidance counsellor asked if it was hard to take care of the house myself.

"We have a really small lawn," I said. "And there's a big tree so the grass doesn't grow very quickly. It's fine."

She shook her head. "I meant cooking, and cleaning, and laundry ... things like that."

"Oh. Right." Mrs. Corcoran, with her neatly bobbed silver-shot hair, the personalized L.L. Bean tote she brings to school, and the framed quote on her desk, saying, **Every day starts as a good day, and you and I can keep it that way,** is probably a traditional mom. The kind who tuts and sighs as she picks her kids' socks up off their bedroom floors. The type who makes them balanced lunches to take to school every day.

"It's OK," I said. "My aunt helps."

My aunt's dead, but I knew the guidance counsellor would find the lie more reassuring than the truth that when my parents are home, we all mostly take care of ourselves anyway, and when they're gone things are, if anything, a little easier.

Besides, it's not a total lie. When I was younger – when my aunt was alive – my parents would go on their trips during summers and school holidays, and Gri-gri and I would stay with her at her horse farm, a three-hour drive away, north of Algonquin Park. All that time with her helped me become the person I am now.

Today's crisp temperatures remind me of Thanksgiving rides with her. The season's first frost sending the horses' noses flaring, tails swishing, energy pounding through them. "If you can sit a horse with their blood up from the cold, you can do just about anything," she told me.

I'd feel a lot different about this cold snap if I had a trip to Turner Bay Stables to look forward to. But whereas my aunt, Ginny Turner was an amazing horsewoman – once even competing for Canada in the Pan-Am Games – she wasn't a great businesswoman. She didn't look after herself very well either, so after her far-too-young heart-attack death, there was no option but to sell the farm. The tech multi-millionaire who bought it as a getaway from her busy city life was also a horse-lover, and graciously agreed to let my aunt's old retirees live out their lives in the pastures they knew, but I couldn't fault her for making the place private.

I wouldn't want to go back anyway. Not without Aunt Ginny there.

The massive double-doors of the school looming in front of me snap me back to the here and now. *I'm doing fine*, I tell myself. I hit everything on my list this morning – walk Gri-gri. Feed both of us. Wash my breakfast dishes. Shower, get dressed ... and still get to school with ten minutes to spare.

All that, of course, after my morning run. It was non-negotiable today, and it will be, no matter how cold it gets, or how much snow falls. Because lots and lots of girls who horseback ride have parents who will drive them to the barn. Who'll pay for them to own or lease a horse. Who will sign them up for private lessons.

But most of them don't think like athletes. None of them run as far, or as hard, or as often, as me.

That's my edge, and I might lose it if things were too easy for me.

Chapter Two

On the days I can't ride, my Fit for Life class is the highlight of my day. It gives me a credit for working out, it's the last class of the day, Mr. Wayne is my favourite teacher, and – the cherry on top of the ice cream sundae – my friend Dana is in it.

Dana and I shouldn't be friends – we're far too different even for people who believe opposites attract. She hates sweating, dairy products, and horses. She loves fermented food, gaming, and wearing high heels.

During the first week of grade nine, I was walking home behind her, wondering what kind of prissy, sissy girl would wear pink patent-leather ballroom shoes to high school, when those shoes stopped square in front of me and she turned to face me. "Help me," she ordered.

I watched as she knelt down next to a squirrel crouching uncharacteristically still by the side of the road.

I mentally took back the "prissy" and "sissy." Give me a horse any day. They don't scare me a bit. But quick-as-a-wink, loudly chattering, sharp-toothed rodents are another story. In my opinion, no human should ever be within touching distance of a squirrel. When Dana reached out and scooped this one up, she earned my respect for life.

Also, putting animals first. That pretty much overcomes any other difference we have.

The squirrel got a fresh chance at life thanks to Dana and the Wild Animal Rescue centre, and I got a fresh new friendship that's endured all through high school ... which, in a hormone-rich, emotionally volatile, teenage environment is not nothing.

In Fit for Life I lift weights, try to achieve and hold difficult stretches, and find new routes across the school bouldering wall. Dana spots me, refills my water bottle, and calls, "Rather you than me!" from her place on the gym mats.

When I complete my traverse and drop to the mat, Mr. Wayne is standing beside Dana. "You're up next," he tells her.

"I don't think so," she says.

He sighs. "Why did you sign up for this course if you were never going to participate?"

Dana's as straight-up as they come – even when it might help her cause to lie a little bit, she just can't. "Ms. Amali told me I need to have some variety on my transcript for my university applications – do something different. So ..." She looks all around her and shrugs, indicating being in this gym is about as out-there as she can imagine.

"Right," Mr. Wayne says, "but I think she meant you should actually *do* the different thing."

Dana lifts her eyebrows. "I'm not so sure about that. She definitely didn't say those exact words." Dana wants to be a lawyer. She's going to be a good one. She's lawyering Mr. Wayne about the course she's taking to improve her chances of eventually getting to law school.

If I can distract Mr. Wayne for three more minutes the bell will ring, and Dana will be home free. "Dana's a team player. Teamwork." I nod, slowly, to show due respect to Mr. Wayne's favourite word. He has one of those cheesy posters on the wall that spells T-E-A-M vertically, with, **Together Everyone Achieves More** coming from the letters.

His brow furrows. "How do you figure?"

"Just now, I wouldn't have made it across without her encouragement."

"Is that so?"

"Absolutely. Her presence gives me strength."

Before Mr. Wayne can call bullshit, Dana holds up my Nalgene. "And I'm going to go fill Laney's water bottle for her. I know how important hydration is." No sooner has she turned on her heel, than the bell rings. "Oh!" she tosses the bottle back to me. "Gotta run! See you later, Laney!"

The rest of the class is right on Dana's heels.

Not me, though. Ever since Mr. Wayne realized I was the student he's been waiting for – the one who truly wants to be as fit as possible, the one willing to be physically uncomfortable to improve my performance – he's been willing to stay for an hour after school to serve as my taxpayer-funded personal trainer.

Which is good, because I don't have the funds for a private one.

"Do that again," he says as I lie, side-planking on a mat that smells of high school gym – a combination of dust, old varnish, and boy sweat. The smell of my second home. After the barn.

I can't. The words that jump into my head are half true. I don't *want* to do another side plank – that's completely true. But I can probably struggle up into some semblance of a plank. I smother a sigh – because Mr. Wayne has a family, and a life, and there are things he'd rather be doing, too – and instead I grunt, because he doesn't mind that, it shows I'm trying. I get myself up ... ish.

Not very straight, it has to be said. Not steady – not at all – in fact, I sway and collapse, much faster this time than the initial attempt which led to his request for a repeat.

He crouches beside me. "So, what's going on here?"

I roll onto my back. "Weakness."

"Where?"

"Core is the most obvious candidate. But ..."

"But what?" he asks.

"Could it be my hip flexor?"

"You tell me."

I rethink my failed side plank. The sense of instability that sent me toppling onto my front. My inability to restabilize. I blink up at him. "The foot bone's connected to the ankle bone ..."

He smiles. Nods. "I agree."

It's something he's taught us all in Fit for Life. Taught me, in particular, in these workout sessions. The pain in your shoulder probably doesn't initiate in your shoulder. Your knee buckles because of weakness elsewhere.

Most of us have a weak spot. Or a tight spot. Or a spot that's weak because it's tight. In my case, ever since I fell off a very clever, very (swervy) pony who deked west and left me deking east, my hip has been creakier than it should be in a teenage body. When I work on my hip, my knees move better, my feet don't hurt, and if I keep it up maybe – just maybe – I'll be able to hold a better side plank.

And in my case the connections go further than the foot bone, connecting to the ankle bone, connecting to the leg bone, because in my case, I want to be able to climb on a one-thousand-pound animal and persuade it to do what I want it to using not much more than my leg and hip bones.

"So, what can we do to work on it?" I ask, and Mr. Wayne says, "Let's figure that out."

Chapter Three

IT'S NEVER TOO COLD to cycle.

I keep telling myself that.

Still, it would help if I had a thicker set of gloves. In the meantime, I flex my fingers to keep them from stiffening around the handlebars. And soon I'm going to have to dig my thermal skull cap out to keep my ears warm under my bike helmet. Having said that, the temperature is above freezing, so my ears might sting a little, but there's no chance of frostbite.

Overall, I'm not going to complain. The ride to the barn might be chilly, but it's a lot quicker than the bus, and the days are coming when it will be too snowy to bike, so I'm going to appreciate cycling while I can.

Plus, it counts as cross-training.

One of the selling points of McKellar Equestrian Park is that it's located within the city limits. The big, rumbling city garbage trucks pick up trash and recycling from the end of the long driveway, which is also where the bus stop is located, and the municipal bike trails run behind the paddocks.

Still, the people who keep their horses here don't come by bike or bus. McKellar's other selling point is the level of comfort it provides – indoor bathrooms, change rooms with showers, the biggest indoor arena in the region (and the only heated one), a conveyor system to clear away dirty bedding and uniformed stable staff to clean the stalls. The parking lot features a couple of stations to let people charge their large, all-wheel drive electric SUVs – it certainly doesn't have a bike rack.

I wheel my bike around to the back of the groundskeeper's shed and lock it to a small maple tree, leaving my helmet hooked over the handlebars. I'll cross the parking lot on foot, heading into the barn just like I'm any other rider arriving in my parents' luxury SUV, or a zippy little car I got for my sixteenth birthday.

The gig I have going here is based on me walking a fine balance. On making just the right impression. It was my Aunt Ginny who first made me realize I could be paid to ride instead of paying – if I played my cards right.

She might have been bad with numbers, but she knew that after the charges for board and lessons, her next biggest earner was the training rides her boarders paid for when they went away to their cottages for weeks at a time or took a summer tour through Europe. As she got older and less fit and I became a stronger rider, she assigned more and more of those training rides to me. It was a dream come true – climbing up on top-class show horses, sourced and schooled by my aunt for her clients – not only riding them for free but being paid to do it.

"Don't you ever pay to ride," she told me one day as I galloped a huge blood-bay Trakehner around her cross-country horse. The horse had a jet-black mane, four long white socks, and the ability and desire to fling himself over all my aunt's big prelim-level jumps. "Do you know the difference between you and this horse's owner?"

I could think of a few. Madeleine's parents drove her out to ride several times a week in a Jaguar, for one. The riding boots she used for everyday schooling were worth more than my bicycle for another. But I was sure my aunt had a point to make so I just kept quiet and let her make it.

"Both you and Madeleine can get this horse clean over these jumps," my aunt said, "But she pays to ride him – not just his original purchase price, but also his board, month-in, month-out – and you get paid to ride him when she's away."

"Take him down the bank, then over the rolltop," she ordered. I felt the immense power of the horse's hind end, his responsiveness at the bottom when I picked up my contact and asked him to focus on the next jump, and the joy that flowed through both our bodies as we cleared it.

I would have given any money I had for that experience, but Aunt Ginny was right, I was being paid to take him around the course, and considering I didn't have the money to pay for it – mostly because my parents didn't think horseback riding was something worth spending money on – I should have my cake and eat it too.

Ride and be paid for it.

It's just one of the many gifts my aunt gave me, and not forgetting it is one of my ways of honouring her memory.

"Hello, luv." As I walk through the parking lot, I come across Scilla lifting bags out of the back of her hatchback. So many bags, every time she comes to the barn – I've learned if you're a horse person with a car, there's no end of sacks of apples, and carrots, and freshly-laundered saddle pads, and dry-cleaned horse blankets you can schlep back and forth.

It's another silver lining of only riding other people's horses – the only thing I have to show up with is my helmet.

I hold out my arms and Scilla drapes a mid-weight taupe blanket with bright turquoise trim over them. "Nice colours," I say.

She nods. "Won't they look lovely on Luna?"

I picture the pop of blue against her warmblood mare's smooth dark coat. "Absolutely."

"The Horsery was having a sale, and this one was in Luna's size. She doesn't have a blanket quite this weight."

I cast my mind over the five other blankets in Luminance's tack locker. I suppose if you scientifically measured each of them, none would be this *precise* weight, so I nod and say, "Great find, then." It's clear to me that Scilla's elegant, retired show jumper is her joy, and far be it from me to interfere with the time or money she spends on her.

I ride Luna twice a week, which supposedly is because Scilla doesn't have enough time, but since she's almost always here when I ride the mare, I think it has more to do with Scilla's generous nature, which I first came into contact with at my aunt's funeral. Scilla sought me out and took me literally under her wing, circling her arm around my shoulders and saying, "Ginny was one of my dearest friends. In fact, she was the one who found my mare for me nearly twenty years ago. She told me what a promising rider you are. I do hope you can ride my special girl for me."

Not only has Scilla's support led me to riding Luna regularly, she's also helped me set up a regular catch riding gig.

Now I lead the way to her tack locker. "Do you want the blanket in the locker?" I ask.

"Sure, for now. Then we can surprise her with it when the temperature drops a little more."

Luna has a big, bright corner stall right across from the tack lockers. She watches us approach with her wide-set eyes and her perfectly tapered and pricked ears, which lend a calm and interested air to her delicately etched face. As long as I've known Luna, I've never known anything to surprise her.

Still, the customer's always right ... except when they're wrong, which is another thing my Aunt Ginny taught me, but a good, kind customer like Scilla is always right.

"Any rides other than this pretty girl?" Scilla's busy feeding carrots to Luna and her neighbours while I fold the new blanket into a corner of the locker.

"I'll check now," I say.

After Scilla decided to be my guardian angel, she put a small metal box labeled *Laney* on a shelf in her locker. Scilla makes sure all new boarders at McKellar know they can leave $25 in cash, their horse's name, riding instructions, and their tack locker's combination in the box and I'll school their horse for them.

It's cheaper than the $45 Becky, the barn manager, charges for training rides and, unlike the working students Becky puts up, I always work on what they ask me to, and leave notes detailing how the ride went.

I open the box and say, "That new flea-bitten grey mare. Her owner says she's stiff on the right rein. She wants me to do lateral work with her, mostly at the trot."

"Why don't you ride her first, while it's still light out and you can use the sand ring? Then I'll watch you ride Luna indoors later."

I know what she's saying. She's saying, *Only ride indoors while I'm there.* Becky is not my biggest fan, and this is her afternoon to teach in the arena.

From the first day Scilla invited me out to ride Luna, Becky has disliked me. "This is a private establishment," she told me, when she came across me grooming Luna in the aisle.

I had opened my mouth to say something placating, when Scilla had popped out of the tack room. "Oh, hello, Becky dear. I see you've met Laney. She's going to help make sure Luna gets the exercise she needs."

The smile Becky forced to her face was as wooden as the jump standards in the arena, "Just looking out for the horses."

"Much appreciated," Scilla had answered. "That's what we're all doing, isn't it?"

As soon as she was out of earshot, Scilla turned to me. "She's always been an awkward girl, and it's worse right now because she's trying to prove to her parents that they made the right decision turning the management of this place over to her. I'm sure she'll come around."

Maybe Scilla would have been right if Becky hadn't come across me tacking up somebody else's horse – a rotund red roan with a biting and kicking streak whose owner wanted me to "remind him of his manners."

I would have welcomed a wooden smile, but what I got was a deep scowl. "Excuse me ..." she said, with a tone that suggested what she really meant was, *What the hell?*

Scilla had popped out from I-don't-know-where – I didn't even know she was at the barn that day – to say, "It's just marvellous for us boarders to have a strong rider like Laney who can help us enjoy our horses so we can keep riding ... and paying board."

Becky had removed the scowl and mumbled, "Yes, of course," but as she walked away, I could see her fists clenching and unclenching.

Since then, she and I have maintained a détente. I avoid tacking up and riding horses in front of her – it's not that I pretend I don't do it, but I figure the less it's in her face, the better – and she settles for sharp reminders of the barn rules when she can catch me breaking them. Like the time I fed a carrot to the red roan, and she informed me that the only people allowed to feed horses are barn staff and each horse's owner.

Now I'm careful to only feed carrots to my mounts when we're alone.

I slip one to the flea-bitten grey when the aisle is empty, then settle the saddle on her narrow back. I run my hand under the saddle and look at it from the front and the back – sticking a few fingers into the withers and gullet areas. There's nothing immediately obvious that would cause her to favour one side, so I'll see how she goes when I'm on her back.

I lead her into the sand ring with about half an hour of decent light left in the day. We pass the first ten minutes getting to know each other and making sure she's properly warmed up, and I spend the next ten asking her to do what she doesn't want to.

At this point I'm not prepared to fight her. I circle her, ask for an inside flexion. She gives it willingly to the left, resists to the right. Fine. We'll go left again, then serpentine. She's beautifully round on the two outside loops, stiff and square on the inside one.

Never stop moving.

She spirals all the way in on the left rein, holding herself nicely, moving into a tiny circle. To the right she's clumsy and stiff and I can hardly get her to do a ten-metre circle.

Now I understand the lay of the land. It's not her saddle. I don't think it's her bit, which seems well-fitted and an appropriate strength. It's not me, because Luna is actually (ever so slightly) stiff to her *left* when I ride her.

I'm ready to start tackling the problem. I dismount.

She sighs. Her ears relax. *Perfect.* I dig into my pocket for the small handful of sweet feed I hid there (thank goodness Becky's not around) and I let her whiffle a couple of grains off my palm. "Good girl."

I move my hand to her left shoulder. No hesitation. She dips her head sideways and takes the offered sweet feed. Next, to the right. We've already established she likes the sweet feed, and wants the sweet feed, so her slower reach for the treat on this side is telling.

If reaching for sweet feed on her right side is a pain, no wonder she doesn't want to flex around a circle.

I pat her neck. "That's fine, girl. Slow and steady. We'll sort you out."

We start with several more right-shoulder touches from the ground, then move into shoulder fore in walk, and finally the trot. Our third try is very good, so I scratch her withers, give her a couple of minutes of good, strong long-reined trot, then gather up the contact for one more, short-but-quite-successful shoulder fore, then let her walk on a loose rein back to the barn.

As usual I think, *I'd do this for free.* I form quick bonds with these horses, and I love the challenge of working on their issues (except with horses like the truly bad-tempered and very lazy red roan). Sometimes I feel guilty pocketing their owners' cash.

But they'd have to pay Becky more to have her assign her not-that-competent working student to ride their horse. And I leave really detailed notes – like I will about the work I did on this mare. And I need the money.

At least I do if I'm going to keep riding.

Chapter Four

McKellar might be close to the city, and McKellar might be posh, but McKellar doesn't have a big-name coach, or a top-class reputation to justify the board they charge.

The stable started as a government initiative – a sporting facility aimed at girls to balance out all the hockey rinks built for boys, back in the day when governments had money they were looking to spend. They built it big, and nice, and comfortable, but it never had cachet.

Then girls started playing hockey, and soccer, and taxpayers started wondering why their money was going to run an equestrian facility, and the government was delighted to sign it over to Becky's parents – a couple of successful local businesspeople with a horseback-riding daughter.

They thought they could run it well, turn a profit. And they did, but it still never had cachet.

That's what Becky wants, now. But despite the barn perched up on a hill with a view of the city, and the big, gleaming tack rooms, and her heated office, prestige isn't something you can manufacture.

So, Becky imports it. She hosts large shows here, with big prize money. She set up an equestrian "boutique" in what used to be a storeroom – selling brands you can't buy anywhere else in the region.

And, once a week, she allows boarders to invite outside coaches in. Sometimes they're trainers with specializations in areas like dressage, or vaulting, or, once, it was polo. For the most part it's high-powered ones – former, or up-and-coming Olympians, or coaches who hold the top coaching certification you can earn in Canada. There's only one of those in our area – Drew, from Stonegate – and he's here almost every week. I always hang around the arena when he's here, watching and learning everything I can.

Today I rushed out after school to get in my ride on the flea-bitten grey mare – who's already improving – so I could ride Luna in the back half of the arena while Drew taught in the front.

As I lead Luna up to the door, a woman with a broom pauses her sweeping. Marge – the backbone of the stable. Becky could be MIA for a week and all the horses would get fed and turned out, and the place would be clean as long as Marge was here. She knows everything that goes on, so when she says, "He's not here tonight," my heart sinks. Marge would know.

"Really?" I wrinkle my nose. "On a buying trip? Coaching a rider at a big out-of-town show?"

She shakes her head. "Trip with his wife. Even riding coaches have personal lives."

I think of Becky, always haunting the aisles here, ready to swoop in at the slightest sign of any misdemeanour. *I wish she had a personal life.* I decide not to say it, though. Marge is great, but Becky signs her paycheque.

"... Jensen's here, though."

I stop thinking about Becky, fast. "Did you say Hilly Jensen?"

"Yup. That 'cretia girl's parents called her in as a 'purchasing consultant.'" Marge gives the words air quotes. She snorts. "I could tell them which horse to buy for that girl of theirs, but it sounds better coming from an Olympian."

I grin. "Anytime you find a horse I can afford, I'll take it on your say-so."

She laughs, then hauls the door open for me, yelling, "Door!"

"Thanks, Marge." I was bracing myself for Becky's dirty look if I opened the door at the wrong time. Nobody questions Marge, though.

"Any time," she says. "In you go and enjoy the show."

As I'm warming Luna up at the far end of the arena where nobody can accuse me of getting in the way of the Olympic consultant, one of Becky's students rides her big chestnut gelding into stride beside me.

Unlike Becky, her students don't have any problems with me. I braid for most of them before shows. Forty-five dollars for a mane, twenty-five for a tail, sixty for both. Beats Becky's eighty-five-dollar price. And I do a better job than the woman she brings in.

"Psst ..." Polly whispers. "You know that's Hilly Jensen?"

I look across to a small group consisting of Becky, two people I recognize as Lucretia's parents, and Hilly Jensen, with a distinctive profile that makes her easily identifiable even without her red Canada jacket and her maple-leaf embossed helmet. "Two gold medals," I say.

Polly nods. "Lucretia's parents inherited some money. She told me they're buying two new horses – one for her to show next season, and one to go into training with Hilly for her to move onto later on."

I watch Lucretia trotting circles on the pretty Paint mare she's had for less than two years. Lucretia's a nice girl with a good basic position. She's not, however, a strong rider, and with Becky as her regular instructor, she hasn't improved in the time I've known her. Her mare knows her job, and they get their fair share of ribbons, but my impression is everything comes easily to Lucretia.

Like two new horses, one trained by Hilly Jensen.

I'm thinking that I want to stay and watch Hilly try these horses, and I'm thinking that I really can't because I have to cycle home. I'm trying not to be bitter about Lucretia with her inheritances, and new show horses, when Polly does it for me. "Obviously money can buy you a lot, but it's never going to make Lucretia a national-level competitor."

I might be able to resist the temptation of piling my opinion onto Polly's – just barely – but I can't muster the magnanimity to contradict her, so I just say,

"I'd better get on with my ride, and you'd better get back before Becky tears her eyes away from Hilly and notices you're fraternizing with the enemy."

I was hoping to at least see part of the trial rides while schooling Luna, but no such luck. I've cooled her out and the only thing that's happened is that Lucretia has left the arena with the Paint mare. The Becky-Hilly-parental huddle is still in full swing.

When I lead Luna back to her stall, Scilla's there with a laundry basket of clean saddle pads and blankets. "I hear there's a bit of gold in the arena tonight," she says.

I nod. "I was hoping to see some of the action, but they're taking their sweet time."

"Right." Scilla lifts the saddle clear of Luna's shiny back. "Let's finish this together and get in there to watch."

"This is my job," I protest.

Scilla shakes her head. "Look at this mare. This time last year she would have been steaming, with her saddle pad soaked through. You've given her a good ride and she's hardly damp. You've taken years off her. I owe you."

I open my mouth, and she continues. "And I want to see if your aunt's eye for a good horse rubbed off on you. Let's see if you and Hilly choose the same horses."

We sit in the corner bleachers and watch Hilly and Lucretia get up on a parade of interesting horses. A couple are horses the stable owns, which explains the sharpening of Becky's eye when Hilly rides them – commission. The rest have been shipped in specially for this trial.

I wouldn't necessarily choose the ones Hilly says she likes, but we'd be looking for different things, and I can see why she goes for them. There are no bad choices here.

I look at the time, then look up at the seventeen-hand, near-black Irish Sport Horse that's just been led in. I'd give my eye teeth for a horse like that and would give a lot to watch him go now, but I should have left half-an-hour ago.

Scilla whispers, "I took my bike in for its end-of-season tune-up a couple of days ago. It fit in my hatchback. I bet yours would too."

I open my mouth to say, *No, thank you*. Scilla already does so much for me – she doesn't have to do this as well.

Then I imagine a voice that sounds suspiciously like my aunt's: *You're right, and she's doing it anyway. Be gracious, girl.*

What's wrong with me? On the one hand, I bemoan the fact that Lucretia has things so easy. On the other hand, every time Scilla tries to make life easier for me, I feel a guilt-driven reluctance to accept her help.

So, instead of saying *no, thank you*, I smile and say, "Thanks. I *would* like to see this one."

Chapter Five

My bike has a flat.

My bike has a flat and I still haven't put the garbage out – but I can hear the garbage truck rumbling on the next street over – and Gri-gri is sitting on the front porch, waiting for his walk like the sweet gentleman he is. When I reach into the mailbox to get the shed key so I can get the bicycle pump, the box yields under the slight pressure of my hand, swinging loose on one side where the screw has pulled free of the rotten wood underneath.

Normally living by myself is fine. Some days everything piles up. Especially, for some reason, on days when I have to be somewhere – like today. Scilla's registered me to ride Luna in two classes at today's circuit show taking place at McKellar.

It's true I have a dozen things to do here. And it's true that it's a long, cold bike ride for just two flat classes.

But I can't let Scilla down.

It's also true that Scilla would come and pick me up if I asked, but the woman does enough for me. She's my personal equitation enabler. I can't ask her to be my taxi as well.

Between people who aren't available for help – my parents – and people I don't want to ask for help, I'm on my own and I'm just going to have to figure things out.

First: garbage to the curb – I can't miss the truck.

Second: walk Gri-gri – it's the least I can do before leaving him for the day.

Third: fix my bike – or I'm not getting anywhere.

Later: figure out the mailbox. Low priority. We only ever get junk mail and bills, and I can find some other equally not-very-secure place to store the shed key.

I'm rolling the garbage can down the driveway under Gri-gri's watchful eye, telling him, "One minute and we'll go for a walk. I'm sorry – it's going to have to be a bit quick, but I'll take you on an extra-long one when I get back, even if it's dark … hey, where are you going?"

My well-behaved dog has bounced up, tail wagging, and jumped off the porch. My heart thumps as I scan the road to make sure the garbage truck hasn't turned onto our street, and my eyes fall on Dana. "What are you doing here?"

"Coming to give your dog a super-long walk while you get going to your show … and using your dining room table to study for my Anthro test, if that's OK."

Another reason Dana and I have such a successful friendship is that we each have something the other needs. Living in a three-bedroom house with five younger brothers and sisters, she needs peace and quiet. Spending as many waking hours as possible at the barn, I frequently need a dog-sitter.

"You know it's OK, but what about babysitting?" The thing about having five younger siblings is that sometimes Dana can't retreat to my house, even when she wants to. Today she was supposed to take care of the five, seven, and nine-year-olds, while her parents took the twelve and fourteen-year-olds to two different hockey tournaments.

"Chicken pox!" She claps her hands. "They all have it so I'm free!"

"I'm sure I shouldn't be happy about it, but I'm glad you're here."

She waves her hand. "Don't worry about it. My mom's glad. She's been holding off on getting them the chicken pox vaccine, so now, mission accomplished – herd immunity in one fell swoop."

"You've saved me from a disastrous morning. I was behind on the garbage, I broke the mailbox, and I was about to shamefully neglect my ever-patient dog."

Dana gathers up Gri-gri's trailing leash, dangles her copy of our house key so I can see it, and says, "I'll take him now. You get going. I'll stay with him until I have to leave for work at three."

"You're an angel!"

She laughs. "No, Gri-gri's an angel. Aren't you, baby? Aren't you?" My dog dances off with his favourite dog-sitter and I clamp the pump onto my bike tire.

***

Show karma is smiling on everybody today. The sunny skies and lack of wind make the temperature moderate for this time of year. It feels like payback for that long stretch in July when the high was above thirty degrees three weekends running, and the horses' hooves sounded like drumbeats on the baked and unforgiving ground. Or for the weekend in August when the skies finally opened to ruin saddles, show the leaks in trailer roofs, and churn the sun-scorched earth into a slippery morass, sending multiple riders and a couple of horses to an unplanned, slithering mud bath.

Still, as I swing my bike through the gate and cruise through the long rows of parked trailers, there's no shortage of winter gear. There's a trendy new brand of long winter riding coat that's been on all the equestrian style blogs, and every second person I pass is wearing one, along with the latest rage in rubber boots – thick-soled, brightly hued, with custom fleece liners you can order to match your stable colours.

Unseasonably warm temperatures aren't going to stop the equestrian crowd from showing off their cold-weather couture.

I don't have the budget or the inclination to spend that much money on new, sport-specific seasonal gear, but I am enough of a conformist that once

I've locked my bike up behind the barn, I peel off my dad's shapeless, patched outdoor pants which are warm, waterproof, and big enough to pull on and off right over my boots, but are undeniably ugly.

A quick glance in at Luna's stall, shows the well-mannered mare conserving her energy in the midst of a barn buzzing with nervous horses and short-tempered riders. She has a hind leg cocked, eyes half-closed and, angel that she is, has neither rubbed out any of her braids, nor rolled in any manure.

I continue to the bathroom and shut myself into a tiny cubicle to complete my transformation from weekend-warrior cyclist to Saturday show girl. My bike helmet and puffy jacket join my dad's discarded shell pants in my big backpack, which I'll stow in Scilla's locker. I shrug into my show jacket and decide the mild temperatures mean I don't need the insulated vest I brought.

When I step out and look in the mirror, I see a girl very much like all the other girls swarming around the property. They might have been driven here, already dressed, by supportive parents. Or they might have changed in the dressing room of a fancy horse trailer. But on the surface, nobody can tell the difference between them and me.

As long as I don't run into Ashley Waverley, that is. Her name's still sewn into the second-hand jacket I bought at the tack swap at the beginning of the season. I heard she went to university this fall, though, so I think I'm clear.

The judges don't know either. It's my aunt's voice, which I can still hear sometimes when I'm lucky. *You ride the way you can, and get that mare to go the way she can, and nobody will be looking at your jacket.*

My phone buzzes with a text: **I brought those boots for you to try.** It's from Hafsa, a girl in my homeroom at school, who rides at a different barn. She just got new boots for her birthday and told me she'd bring her old ones today so I could try them. "If you like them, I'll sell them to you."

"I appreciate it," I'd said. "But I'm not sure if I'll be able to afford them."

"I'll give you a good price," she said.

The right thing to do would probably be to tell her there's no chance and say *thanks but no thanks* on trying them.

But I've seen them and they're gorgeous. The leather is buttery soft and gleams with good care. They make Hafsa's ordinary calves look long, and lean, and strong.

If Hafsa's willing to let me show in them today, I'm not about to say no.

I sometimes wonder if I notice the sounds, smells, and sights of shows more than other people because I'm not able to take them for granted. I slow as I pass the warm-up ring, watching riders being schooled by their coaches. I wonder what that's like – to have someone looking out for you, muscling in so you get a turn over the warm-up jump, telling you (even if it's not true) that you're ready for your class, noticing small details like a smudge on your boot, or a wisp of hair escaping from under your helmet.

Then again, maybe it would bug me. I'm used to hollering "heads up over the X!" on my own behalf. To "borrowing" the big mirrors on the six-horse trailers to catch any splats of mud or stray shavings.

"Coming through!" A white-faced girl on a horse with his chin cranked to his chest, veins standing out on his neck, and red showing around his nostrils, plunges by so close I can hear her whispering, *please, please, please* under her breath. The horse snorts, and she moans.

"Bring him here," her coach calls from a spot off to the side of the warm-up jumps. It's Drew, who I wanted to watch earlier in the week

"I can't." Her voice is a whimper, too quiet for him to hear.

"Vanessa! Put your heels down, sit in your saddle, and ride that horse over here."

Despite her uncertainty and her lack of confidence I watch her do just that. Drew looks the horse over, then runs a cloth over the horse's face, and the girl's boots. He talks to her for a minute, using two fingers pointed at her eyes, then his, to insist on eye contact.

She picks up her reins, rides the horse into a beautifully round circle, then clears the closest warm-up jump as though it's a pole on the ground.

I've seen this girl ride before. She isn't that talented. She's clearly not that keen about being here. The horse is gorgeous, but I happen to know the reason he's competing here is because he couldn't cut it at a higher level. Mid-level horse and rider. Low motivation. Yet, I watch them clear another jump in ribbon-winning style.

There's a reason Drew has a waiting list, and why there's never an empty stall at his barn, Stonegate, even though he doesn't have a heated arena like the one here *and* the board is two hundred dollars a month higher.

I push away from the fence and head off to find my second-hand boots, with visions of Stonegate's tree-lined driveway, white-railed fields, and Intermediate-level cross-country course dancing in my head. Who needs a heated arena when you have all that, and the best coach for hundreds of kilometres?

The giggling tells me I'm at the right place. Hafsa's giggling, to be exact. I'm sure, just like the rest of us, Hafsa has problems, anxieties, and issues ... but you'd never know it. She's always friendly, smiling, laughing. She's a person who's nice to be around and obviously the group of girls gathered around her feels that way, too.

They're all wearing white breeches with riding socks pulled up to their knees. Each pair of socks is different, but they're all colourful and whimsical – meant to be noticed – so in that way they're all the same. Each of them wears a pink toque with a gold logo that reads, "Pippa Chadwick Equestrian." Hafsa is different in that her glossy black hair stands out in a sea of highlighted platinum, and because she's clearly the centre of the group.

"Laney!" She sounds both delighted to see me, and genuine. A rare combination. "The boots are in the trailer dressing room. Try them on in there if you like – it's warm inside." She takes a step forward, but I can't bear to make her leave her admirers.

"That's great – thanks! You don't need to come."

She smiles. "Okey-dokey. Just let me know if you need anything."

Hafsa is one of the only people I know who can say, "okey-dokey" without sounding completely cringe-worthy.

The giggles start up again even as I'm stepping into the trailer. Would I like that? My own posse of horse-girl friends? Realistically the answer is probably sometimes yes and sometimes no ... what I'm pretty sure I would always like, though, is access to a trailer dressing room like this one.

Just like Hafsa said, it's deliciously warm. It also smells like new carpet and expensive leather.

I sit on an upholstered bench, which I happen to know folds out into a bed, and try to imagine having not only my own horse, but my own trailer. And not just any trailer, but one I could sleep in. Comfortably. Because there's no doubt this trailer is very cozy.

There's also no doubt the boots are gorgeous. For my money, the gentle creases around the ankles, and the patina of the used-and-well-cared-for leather makes them nicer than the stiff, gleaming new ones I saw Hafsa wearing. Which is fortunate, because my money would never stretch to the boots Hafsa has on.

I slide them on, stick my feet out in front of me, admire my legs in the lovely boots and think, *There's no reason I can't win my class in boots like this.*

***

I smooth my hand along Luna's silky neck and lean down to accept the fluttering red ribbon from the smiling local realtor who sponsored the class.

I ride out of the ring and hand the ribbon to a beaming Scilla, along with the envelope that accompanied it. She's now sporting two red ribbons looped over the belt of her coat and has a whopping forty dollars in prize money in the envelopes in her pocket.

What a sport, when the prize money for finishing first is still less than the cost to enter the class. Then again, looking at the pride on Scilla's face, I know it's not about the money.

There's a small rise that gives a nice vista over the showground. We halt Luna there – where, of course, she stands lovely and square – and hook the bright ribbons over the rich leather of her reins, then snap away. Scilla with Luna. Me with Luna. A passerby offers to take a picture of both of us with the mare, and we're just thanking her, when somebody calls out, "Laney!"

It's Hafsa. "Our stable has a horse that needs to be ridden in the Open Jumper Medal. I said I'd ask you – will you do it?"

"Isn't it now?"

Hafsa nods. "The rider just threw her back out in the warm-up ring."

The Open Jumper Medal. As happy as Luna's ribbons have made Scilla, and as nice as it was to hear my name called first … those were just flat classes. I would *love* to ride in the Jumper Medal. "Sorry. I don't know the course—" I lay my hand on the mare's glossy neck "—and I have to put Luna away."

"She'll pay you."

"Excuse me?"

"There's a potential buyer here to see the horse go. She needs him to show. The only place and time he can see the horse is right now, in this class."

I shake my head. "It's not about the money." Which is true. I would definitely ride in the Open Jumper Medal for free … but getting paid to do it as well? That makes it even harder to say no.

"She gave me the money. She'll pay you up front." Hafsa counts out four twenties. She and I both look down at her second-hand boots I'm wearing. She and I both know it's nearly enough for me to buy them from her.

But … I look back at the sweet, patient mare who just carried me to two red ribbons, still tacked up and braided. She deserves a deep grooming, and a bunch of carrots, and some extra bedding in her stall – when Becky's not looking.

The first rule of horsemanship is you take care of your horse first. No matter what. "I'm sorry. I can't."

Scilla takes the reins from me. "You can't not. Off you go. I'll take care of her."

"Scilla …" I start.

"Go!" she orders. "Now! I'll untack her and try to get to the ring in time to see your round. You can pull her braids out after if it makes you feel better."

Chapter Six

I'VE RIDDEN HORSES THIS good before, but I've never showed one. My role has always been to tune them up, condition them, keep them sharp, so their owners can come in on the weekend and ride into the ribbons.

My show experience has mostly been on challenges. Horses that need a firm leg and seat, and a strategic ride so they can maybe grab a ribbon and increase their owner's chances of selling them on to somebody else who will later have trouble showing them.

It's a good thing this horse is so amazing, because most of my focus has been on learning the course. The number one, most unforgivable mess up would be to ride out there and take the horse to the wrong jump. That's an easy one-hundred percent rider fault with nobody caring that the first time I saw the course was five minutes ago.

I seek out clear space near the ring so I can ride the horse in circles – trying to get a feel for his stride, his mouth, his responsiveness – while I watch the riders before me, and mutter under my breath, "Vertical, oxer, triple – one, two, three, liverpool ..." I'm able to do that five times before the gate opens for me.

Smile. It's my aunt's voice again. And she's right. I'm doing this either way – I'm committed – so I might as well trot in with a massive smile and try to fool everyone, and that includes me and my horse.

But really, what is there not to smile about? I can feel every movement of the horse through his high-end, lightweight saddle. And the movements I can feel are strong and rhythmic. The leather of the reins is smooth and supple, as is the mouth of the gelding I'm communicating with. And Hafsa's boots – it's like they were made for me – they let me jam my heels down, giving me a balanced, stable position over the first jump ... which the horse rounds over with ease.

The rest of the course is just as lovely. All I have to do is remember our path over the jumps. This horse is so well-schooled that a simple glance around a corner, my gaze fixing on the next obstacle, fixes his attention, too. I ask him for a fast pace. He gives it to me, keeping his ears pricked forward, eating up the ground, and we finish clear, and quick.

Onto the flat phase, which he also executes perfectly. None of the requirements cause him any trouble. His trot is so smooth it's as comfortable to sit as his walk. He lengthens his stride without quickening. He picks up the canter equally well on both leads and holds the counter-canter without ever making me worry he'll switch.

It doesn't surprise me at all when we win. This morning, I knew Luna was the best in her class, and the same thing was clear with this horse, in this class ... except, as sweet as Luna is, this is a level above her. There are quite a few people watching, as well, including Scilla who beams and shoots me a thumbs-up as I exit the ring.

Hafsa's coach, Pippa, meets us at the gate. "That was amazing – the buyer's taking him on a two-week trial. It was worth every penny to get you to ride him."

I jump off the horse and slide up the near stirrup while Pippa runs up the other one. "I feel a little guilty for taking money for that ride – he just needed somebody to perch on his back."

Pippa meets my eye across the saddle. "Are you kidding me?"

"What?"

"His owner can never get him to take the left lead canter or hold counter-canter."

I furrow my brow. "But he was perfect."

"For *you*," Pippa nods. "Like I say – worth every penny."

"Do you want me to take him back to the trailer?" I ask.

She shakes her head. "Nope. They're taking him on trial right from here. I'll take him over to their trailer."

She walks away with the good-natured horse, cooler throw over his back, red ribbon pinned to his bridle, walking easily beside her. I feel a pang for him – what must it be like to be at the mercy of humans? To come in one trailer and go home in another?

Then again, he's such a lovely horse he should do well wherever he goes, and he deserves a rider who can get him to canter on the left lead.

Meanwhile I head back to Hafsa's trailer to return her boots. Up until an hour ago I was bracing myself to give them back and tell her I just can't afford them. Now I reach into my pocket and feel the twenty-dollar bills there. "The boots are great," I tell her. "I have the rest of the money at home. If you can bring them to school Monday, I'll bring you the cash."

"You can keep them now if you like," she offers.

"I rode my bike, so it would actually be easier if you take them back for me."

She grins. "Absolutely. Your name is golden around here right now. Bridget's at home on painkillers, but I sent video of your round to her. She says you're a miracle worker. Now that Domino's sold she can get her new horse – they're importing him from Belgium."

Well, that takes away my guilt at accepting the eighty dollars from her. "Glad I could help."

I step back into the dressing room – still warm thanks to a tiny space heater humming in the corner. I would have been sad to slide these beautiful boots off if I couldn't buy them, but now it's just a matter of time. I run my hand over the supple leather. "I'll pick you up soon."

As I leave the trailer, I glance back to make sure I haven't left anything behind, leading me to miss a step, lurch to the ground, and smack full force into somebody who is thankfully tall and strong enough not to be knocked over by the contact.

He grabs hold of my arms to steady me. "Forgot your trailer has a step?"

It's not my trailer. I'm stopped from saying it by a wave of inertia. That statement would only lead to another one – to me explaining why I'm in a trailer that isn't mine – and I honestly can't be bothered. Why can't I be like every other rider here? Or, at least, why can't I just let this guy think I am? I'll never see him again, so it doesn't matter.

I'll just pretend this is my expensive trailer, and my expensive horse is being walked by my groom, and I'm off to ... what do girls with lots of spending money do at horse shows?

"It's a new trailer," I say. Which is sort of true. It's new to me – today's the first day I've ever been in it.

He smiles one of those smiles that some people call enigmatic, or even refer to as a Mona Lisa smile (although our art teacher told us about research that says Mona Lisa's expression is actually the same as people who have lost their front teeth, and her face shows signs of blunt force trauma – how's that for a romance killer?).

At any rate, it's true I can't tell what his smile means, and I'm fairly sure he's at least partly laughing at me. I file it under "infuriating," and avoid meeting his eyes by pretending to focus on smoothing the front of my jacket. It puts me a second behind in registering his question to me. "You going to watch the Capital Medal Final?"

The truth is, I was going to check in on Luna, thank Scilla, then get on my bike and head home.

"Yes," I say. Because that's what the rich girl I'm pretending to be would do, and I feel like being her for a little longer. Especially because the cheekbones above that enigmatic-frustrating smile are very chiseled and, also, its owner's teeth are lovely and white and even. No hint of Mona Lisa there.

I'm glad I left my bike helmet in Scilla's locker. I've never seen a rich-girl rider carrying a bike helmet around.

***

We're about to climb onto the metal bleachers when a girl says, "Hey, Darce, take this for me, would you?"

She doesn't say please, and she doesn't wait for him to answer before hauling the quarter sheet off the back of her horse and tossing it to Cheekbones.

I want to say, *Nice manners*, but the familiarity in her tone says they have some connection – stablemate, sister, girlfriend *(fingers crossed, not girlfriend)* – so I bite my tongue.

He gives me a different version of his smile. This one seems to be holding back laughter. Then he winks and says, "I don't know about you, but I don't particularly enjoy the sensation of cold aluminum under my backside." With a flick of his wrist, he unfurls the quarter sheet across an area of the bench wide enough for both of us, then says, "After you."

It's a gorgeous quarter sheet – the wool is thick and soft – and he's right that it beats cold, hard metal any day.

Something about his grin, and his willingness to use the girl's expensive blanket as a butt-warmer, makes me think I don't have to worry that he's romantically involved with that particular rider, so instead of asking about her, I wait until he's settled beside me, then say, "Darce?"

He turns to face me, holds out his hand, and says, "Darcey. Yes, I ride horses but that's where the Jane Austen similarity ends."

When I take his hand it's big, strong, slightly rough, and warm. "Laney," I say. "Don't worry. I've always been partial to Frank Churchill."

"Hmm ... I've only seen *Pride and Prejudice*." He lifts his eyebrows. "Although I could possibly be persuaded to give *Emma* a try."

Not only is he hot, but he's willing to watch Jane Austen movie adaptations. That's sexy even if it is a total lie. I let myself imagine snuggling on the couch with popcorn, watching Jane Austen with Darcey ...

"What do you think of this mare?" His question snaps me back to the quarter-sheet-covered aluminum bleachers. It may not be the cozy corduroy couch in our living room, but there wouldn't be horses there, so this will do fine.

I watch the brown mare canter toward the first obstacle, stride steady and ears pricked. She's unfashionable in every sense of the word. Not a leggy off-track Thoroughbred. Not a sturdily athletic warmblood. Not young. Not green. Not flashy. Not tall.

Overall, the best word to describe the 15.2 hands high dull-brown mare with her rounded rump and her hollow neck is nondescript.

"I think they might win," I say.

He lifts one eyebrow. *Oh, now that's cute.* "Really?"

I nod. "She knows exactly what to do, and her rider's smart enough to stay out of her way and let her do it. Plus, this course is perfect for her. Tight and twisty. On wide-open courses she loses out to big horses because of her short stride, but here ..." I lift both my hands, then let them fall. "Perfect for her."

"You seem to know a lot about her."

"I rode her once."

"You did?" He's staring at me now, and I realize I was very close to telling him the truth – that the last time she was sold, her previous owner and new owner agreed she'd be stabled here for her trial period – neutral territory between the old barn an hour east, and the new one, an hour west. Because, apparently, the girl only ever rides twice a week, I exercised the mare on the other days – finding her smart, responsive, and athletic in a cat-like way.

Since that would blow my rich-girl cover, I shrug and say, "It was before this girl owned her."

Which is the partial truth.

"I think most people would choose *them* to win." He points to the girl who owns the quarter sheet currently cushioning my backside, and the deeply dappled grey she's astride.

The mare hasn't relaxed once the whole time I've watched them, but I'm not going to argue. "Hmm ... they certainly look good."

"Oof," he says. "Talk about damning with faint praise. I didn't say *I* thought they'd win." He pauses. "In fact, I agree with your assessment."

It's ridiculous, because it's not like he said anything romantic, or sexy, but his eyes catch and hold mine as he says it, and I don't look away, and I find my heart racing. *I agree.* Maybe that *is* kind of sexy.

In fact … while I'm doing this pretending-to-be-rich thing, maybe I should also entertain pretending-to-have-a-crush-on-a-cute-guy …

A phone rings. Shrill and sudden. He blinks, breaks our eye contact, and says, "Sorry, that's me."

While he takes the call, I shiver – the insulation from the quarter sheet seems to have disappeared.

Phone call over, he turns back. "Apparently one of our clients has a flat, and doesn't know how to change it." He shrugs. "So, that's me."

Oh. So he's not a spoiled, rich rider boy.

He's being honest with me – I should have been honest with him. Also … it wouldn't be the worst thing in the world to see him again. Which I could have done if I'd told him the truth about who I am.

He swings down from the bleachers. "This was fun."

"It was." I nod. *It really was.* I finger the blanket and, for just a second think of staying quiet, letting him forget it so I can use it as an excuse to see him again.

Except, I just figured out that isn't going to happen. I stand and whisk the blanket out from under me. "Don't forget this."

"Oh yeah, thanks." He folds it roughly under his arm. "I would have been in trou-ble if I'd come back without it."

His phone rings again. "I'd better go."

I smile. "Bye." As I watch him walk away, I automatically sink back to the bench, then immediately jump up again as the cold metal jolts through the thin fabric of my show breeches.

That's it. My show day is done. Three red ribbons, a pocket full of cash, and the promise of a beautiful pair of new-to-me boots.

You'd think I'd feel better as I head toward the barn. But in the distance I catch sight of his broad shoulders and straight back heading toward the parking area, and watching him go leaves an empty, flat feeling in the pit of my stomach.

Chapter Seven

IT'S ONE OF THOSE days when life sings. Mr. Wayne has to leave early to run try-outs for the school curling team, so he lets us out of class half-an-hour early. Dana, who has a mid-term she wants to study for in the quiet of my house, walks home with me, so I can leave Gri-gri safe with her and head straight to the barn.

It's unseasonably warm, so I don't even need gloves, and my bike tires hum as I whip by the stop-and-go traffic on the highway that runs parallel to the barn road. *Who'd bother with a car anyway?*

Today it's easy to think that.

There are two names and fifty dollars cash in Scilla's locker. I ride the first one – a youngster who needs to learn how to step over trot poles – and when I bring him back in, find Scilla in the barn wearing breeches. "What do you say we ride out on the cross-country course together?" she asks. "It could be the last hack of the season."

The second horse I've been asked to ride is Luna's paddock-mate, owned by one of Scilla's friends, and the two horses are happy to walk side-by-side across fields tinted gold by the touch of the late-autumn sun.

There's an insulated part of the property – far enough back that the endless rush of cars on the four-lane highway is barely a whisper, a strip of trees blocking any view of the cyclists and dog-walkers on the municipal recreational path – where it's easy to believe we're deep in the country.

And while I'm believing that, I pretend the retired A-Circuit jumper I'm riding is mine. I focus on Scilla's straight back and relaxed elbows, and imagine my aunt isn't dead – that's her, right in front of me, and after we ride, we'll do night check side-by-side, then she'll make me her special mac 'n' cheese for dinner and we'll get up in the morning and ride some more horses together.

I envision my future and it's full of people who can teach me a lot, and horses who can teach me more, and I'll find a way to earn money and ride horses ... I close my eyes, and the bird song, and warm breezes, and sun on my face make it easy to believe.

"What are you doing?" Scilla's voice, so different from my aunt's, jolts me back to reality. My eyes fly open and catch on a raised storm main – so much for being deep in the country – and I notice how close the sun is to the horizon.

My aunt's dead, this horse isn't mine and, despite today's weather reprieve, the days are very short and undeniably going to get colder.

I blink at Scilla. "I was just soaking in the sun."

She smiles. "No dress rehearsal ..." She doesn't need to finish. I know exactly what she means. This is my life and I'm on the back of a horse, on a lovely day, with a kind person, so I'm doing OK.

***

My Zen has slipped a little by the time I climb into the corner bleachers to watch the private lessons. The open square where the arena doors are rolled back is already pitch black against the indoor lighting. And the air it's letting in has cooled quickly with the disappearance of the sun.

There's no denying the snow and ice is coming, which means switching from my bike to the bus, which means less time to ride ...

Also, my soup is lukewarm. If I have to bring my food from home, I at least want it to be hot. I probably need a new Thermos, which is the last thing I want to spend money on, but it's not like I can afford the vegan, organic take-out the girl at the other end of the bleachers wolfed down before hopping on the gleaming, already-tacked-up horse her groom led to her. I watch her mother fold the Chic Chow wrapping – boldly stamped recycled and biodegradable into a neat square. Her wrap probably cost as much as my entire ride fee.

I stop hankering after other people's lives and good fortune when Drew walks in and takes his place at the centre of the ring. He's a strange combination of low-key and high intensity. He enters the ring quietly, his hoodie, worn jeans, and work boots are indistinguishable from the barn staff who muck the stalls and sweep the aisles here, and his voice is low, but the minute he uses it, both his rider and her horse turn their heads to him.

Me, too.

I forget cold soup and the looming winter. I spin right back to my earlier state, pretending I could be the next one to ride a horse coached by this man with his ability to pinpoint weaknesses in a way that makes you squirm first, then fix them fast. And, when you do, his praise is swift and as warming as summer sunshine – even if it's also sparing and doesn't protect you from continued critique.

I'd give a lot for informed critique like that. His current rider, I'm not so sure about. Her nose wrinkles and she blinks a couple of times. She doesn't complain, though, and she tries what he suggests.

She gets about halfway to where he wanted her, then he says, "Good effort. That's enough for tonight," and her chest and shoulders lift. It's not just the horses he can read. He'll get more out of this rider next time because he left her on a positive note.

I'm watching Drew work with his second student of the night. I know this woman – she's a professor at one of the local universities taking a one-year sabbatical and working toward doing her first event this summer. I know her horse, too. I've ridden him a couple of times. He's a lovely, big, sturdy gentleman with his one-quarter Clydesdale heritage showing in his feathery legs. It's fun to see what Drew can get out of this pair I know.

He's made good progress on getting Glasgow to actually swing his long legs and track up in the walk, when my view is obscured by a tall, grey gelding with massive white-edged dapples blooming all over his spotless coat. His tack glows like only very expensive, very clean leather can, and although I've never seen his rider anywhere but the barn, I've also never seen a speck of dirt, flake of shavings, or length of hay anywhere on her clothes or in her hair.

She leans toward me, holding out a twenty-dollar bill. "The usual?"

I zip the twenty into my bag, along with my empty Thermos, and tuck it under the bleachers. "Sure."

She takes my spot on the bench, I take her horse, and before I'm even finished adjusting my stirrups, her thumbs are flying across her phone screen.

I ride her horse to the far end of the arena where I won't interfere with Drew's lesson. It's not like his rider's going to watch, anyway. She told me once that between her competitive swim training, at 5:00 a.m. every day, then all day at private school, back in the pool after school, then straight to the barn, these times that I warm up her horse are often her only opportunity to spend fifteen minutes on her phone. "Plus, I trust you."

Maybe it was the compliment that made me like her. Or maybe it was just the realization that we all have our burdens to bear – even if they're not visible. Most people would have no idea that I'm driven to ride by the unshakeable belief my now-dead aunt had in my ability, and that I'll do just about anything to earn the money to keep doing it.

It's not what they expect when they look at me, so it's not what they see.

That realization makes me happy to cut the girl some slack – that, and the heavenly trot of this horse of hers. "I'm not going to take him to university with me," she told me the last time I warmed him up. "You should buy him."

See? My careful purchases of high-quality second-hand riding gear, and the care I take of them, means she doesn't know there's no way I could ever afford her horse.

Plus ... he's not scrappy enough. This horse is as compliant as a good-natured Golden Retriever. He's been coddled, and cossetted, and pampered since he was a foal – which is great, which is how all horses should be treated.

But they aren't, which means there are horses out there with hang-ups and, for my sins, I quite enjoy riding them.

Still, for now, it's great to know that all I have to do is create a warm-up plan, use my aids correctly, and focus, and the big horse will be fully framed up and flexed within ten minutes.

Drew tells his student to cool down and I take advantage of her coming off the rail to canter the entire arena, both directions. I lengthen on the long sides, collect through the corners, and deliver the horse back to his rider with just the slightest flare to his nostrils, ears pricked, eyes shining, and ready to go.

I'm holding her dressage whip while she adjusts her stirrups when Drew walks over. "Don't you warm up your own horse?"

She places her foot in her stirrup, drops her heel down, and gives him the self-assured look of somebody who doesn't have to worry what other people think about them. "Why would I, when Laney can do it for me?"

Then, as her coach enters the arena, she winks and rides away.

Drew turns to me. "That wouldn't happen at my stable."

I believe him. I also don't know how to answer. In the background, the coach is saying, "Lovely – you've got him going really well." Which, of course, is thanks to my warm up.

"Why would you do that for her?" Drew asks.

I finger the twenty-dollar bill in my pocket but decide not to mention it. Instead, I shrug. "I got to get on that horse." He sweeps by, all shine, and muscle, and power. "Just look at him."

His hoofbeats shake the ground under our feet. Even if I wouldn't buy him, I would pay to ride a horse as good as that – if I had the money. But by working my butt off – by riding every kind of horse that comes along, and getting up and running in the dark when the puddles are frozen solid – I can be good enough that people will pay me to ride their great horses.

I turn to face Drew and say, "Why on earth wouldn't I?"

Chapter Eight

THE CLASSROOMS ARE SO much brighter now that the snow's come, with the white outside reflecting the late-season sunlight through the windows.

Everything, in fact, is brighter, even my pre-sunrise run, with the smooth white blanket on the ground amplifying the light from the moon and the streetlamps.

It makes Gri-gri happy, too – the first snowfall of the year always reverts him to puppy mentality. For a while, anyway. He buries his nose in the fresh drifts, and snorts, then hops and leaps after the explosion of snowflakes he creates.

When I left for school, he was sound asleep after his early-morning snow-chasing exertions.

Someone else excited by the snow is Ms. Brisebois. She calls me as I walk by her desk on my way out of History. "Laney! The first meeting for the cross-country ski team is at lunch. You're so good at cross-country running – I'd love it if you'd come."

"Sure," I say. It makes her happy and it's good cross-training.

I can't keep the snow from falling – can't make it melt, so I might as well make the most of it.

But it doesn't erase the fact that the snow's too heavy for my bike, the plows are struggling to keep up with the first fall of the year, and I'll have to take the bus to the barn tonight.

***

The cold seeps through the fabric of my breeches where my knee is propped against the bus's metal skin. I can feel it through my toque as well, as I tilt my head against the window, trying to find a comfortable angle to read about Canada's history of trade with Castro's Cuba.

I can do this, I tell myself even as the words blur and refuse to sink into my brain. Then, straightening my spine, *Of course I can*. People do harder things every day. I need to keep this in perspective. I'm lucky to be able to ride, even if it requires taking the bus. I'm lucky to ride at a stable that has a bus servicing it ... well, *near* it.

And I've done this before. Just not when I had a grade twelve workload. Never when my parents were out of the country on a months-long sabbatical, and I was responsible for everything at home.

Never in a year when I promised myself I'd get as good as I possibly could so I could become a working student in a high-profile barn and be able to travel to all the biggest shows.

I shift. Move my eyes back to the top of the page. One thing's for sure, I'm never going to accomplish any of it if I can't even get this reading done now.

As it turns out, there's a silver lining to all this snow, because I find a note in Scilla's tack locker asking me to ride a sweet and furry Canadian horse, with his owner writing, *Can you please make sure he's not afraid of the snow?*

I'm surprised at the notion that a horse named for this northern country would be afraid of the snow, but it's not up to me to question the paying clients. When I lead him out the stable door, the young gelding flares his nostrils wide and snorts plumes of hot breath into the cold air, sending snowflakes swirling around his face – maybe this is why she thought he might be scared?

He's not, though. As soon as I swing onto his back and point him at an unspoiled stretch of white, it's clear he's as delighted as I am to be prancing through the soft snow, and bodying through the drifts.

The figure eights we trace start to fill in as soon as we create them. We slide down a slight hill bringing a mini avalanche with us.

When we head back to the barn, I'm cold but in a good way – with pink cheeks and lungs full of fresh air. I've forgotten about school, and responsibilities, and money for a little while. And I can tell the woman, "Don't worry – your horse isn't afraid of snow."

Win-win, I'm thinking as we round the corner back to the barn door and my heart jumps, as does the horse I'm riding, at the unexpected apparition of Becky standing there.

I've managed to avoid her for the last little while. If I hear her voice in the tack room, I walk on by. If she turns down the aisle while I'm getting a horse ready, I duck into its stall. I never, ever go into, or anywhere near the main office.

And now here she is, standing at the door I'm clearly heading for. Something about the way she's holding a big shovel, standing with her shoulders square to me, a dark, solid thing in this snow-globe-like landscape of whiteness and fluffiness makes me shiver, makes my mount stop in his tracks.

There's no way to turn and go to another entrance without it being obvious that I'm avoiding her. And there's nobody else around to diffuse our encounter.

Shit. *Shit-shit-shit.*

I don't want to walk up to her. I don't want to talk to her. But just like on the bus, I remind myself lots of people need to do much more difficult things every day.

Time to remember I'm wearing my big-girl breeches and walk up to Becky.

Except nobody's told my horse. He's not afraid of the snow, but he is afraid of the bulky figure, holding what looks like a weapon, and it doesn't help that, like all horses, he's basically telepathic and I've just sent him some very strong vibes that Becky is Bad News.

He doesn't care about my leg squeezing, or my voice urging, he's not going.

One thing I never do is fight with horses. Neither of us enjoys it, and they weigh up to ten times more than me, so I always get them to do what I want, but not through confrontation.

I hop off his back, run my stirrups up, humming the whole time. Then I stand by his shoulder and step forward like it's no big deal.

And it works. He steps sweetly forward beside me.

See? Just as I'm congratulating myself on my horse whispering abilities, I look up to the door, fake smile plastered to my face, ready to face my enemy ... only to find her gone.

What the ...?

Maybe she just came out to shovel the area around the entrance.

Except, as the horse and I step through the door, we kick a load of snow in with us. No clearing done.

So, for some reason, Becky came out into the snow, glared at me, then went back in without saying anything.

Weird but not unwelcome.

In the last few minutes, I've avoided confrontations with both this horse, and with Becky. I shrug. *Don't look a gift horse in the mouth*, they say.

I guess I'll take that advice.

Chapter Nine

I HAVEN'T GOTTEN AROUND to buying a new Thermos, so tonight I'm eating a sandwich when Drew arrives to start his private lessons.

"I'm relieved you're not warming up my student's horse," he says.

It takes me a second to realize he's talking to me. He recognized me. He remembered.

I laugh. "I wouldn't dare."

What I don't tell him is last summer I rode this very horse for the whole month of July while his rider was on vacation in Europe. Two days after she got back, she rode him in a show, placed in every class, and got Reserve Champion.

Her parents were so happy they paid me a bonus, so there's no chance I'd mention it to Drew – it's a kind of rider-client confidentiality.

The girl and the horse look good together. That show last summer was a turning point. She's been a lot more confident since then. I enjoy watching the lesson. As they cool down, Becky comes to the arena door. She doesn't glance at me, just addresses the arena at large. "Snow's still falling." She looks straight at Drew. "Your next student called to say she can't make it – we're going to call lessons for tonight. It's not safe to ask anyone else to come out the way the roads are."

Marge is standing behind Becky. She speaks over Becky's shoulder to Drew. "Since you're here anyway, why don't you look at that horse we were talking about. It might be a good option for that student of yours who's grown out of her large pony."

Drew looks at his watch, then his eyes find me. "Will you let me put her up on it to see how it goes? My student's about the same size."

It takes me a second to register that he's jutting his chin toward me. I'm the "her" he wants to put up on the horse.

"Sure." Marge gives me a quick smile. "You know the horse," she tells me. "The gelding at the end of aisle two. The mom thought she'd ride him while her daughter was at university but now she and her husband want to travel."

I do know the horse. I also know Marge is probably in line for a commission if she arranges the sale.

Just like last week, I scramble to shove my bag under the bleachers, but this time I'm riding for Drew.

I've ridden lots of horses, for lots of people, under lots of circumstances. I'm mostly past being nervous, but there's a tiny flutter of butterflies in the pit of my stomach as I snug my helmet into place.

I've never ridden the horse, but I've seen him go many times. His show name is First Impression, and I think it fits. He's the right size – about 16.2hh. The right colour – a nice even brown. He frames up the minute I settle on his back.

At first glance he looks good, but I've always wondered if there's any substance to him.

There isn't.

Drew watches me warm him up – trot circles both directions, a forward canter around the ring, then he calls me onto a circle around him. "Keep it big," he orders. "I want you to lengthen. Let me see what he's got."

The answer is, not that much. He's one of those horses who wants to go faster when I ask him to lengthen – not necessarily because he's lazy – more because he doesn't have the scope to propel himself from behind and deliver the suspended strides he needs to.

Similarly, when Drew asks me to collect him, he just wants to bunch up, arch his neck, and mince.

He doesn't have the power needed for either collection or extension. I've felt the real deal before – been lifted by the horse's back, felt like I was floating, but on something much stronger than a cloud. This is not that.

"What do you think?" Drew asks.

I look over at Marge. I feel awkward dissing the gelding in front of her.

"What you see is what you get," I answer.

"Ha!" When he lets it go, Drew's voice rings through the arena. "She's saying your horse is weak."

That's not what I said ...

Before I can say it, though, Marge shrugs. "Hey, he's not my horse, and he won ribbons for his current owner. Besides, I've seen how your potential buyer rides."

Drew nods. "You have a point there. Not everybody needs, wants, or can handle a Lamborghini."

Marge is quick to add, "You have to admit he looks nice right now."

Drew screws his mouth up. "You just said you've seen my student ride." He points at me. "Not quite the same level. Still ..." He cocks his head to the side. Squints. "It might work."

"That's what I said."

"For the right price ..." he says.

Marge taps the arena boards. "You let me know when you're ready to talk money. I can hook you up with the owners."

I've been walking the horse on a long rein during this exchange. Drew nods at me and I slide off. Marge comes out to meet me. She holds her hands out for the reins. I hand them over while I run up my stirrups and loosen the girth.

While I'm on the far side of the horse she asks me, "Hey, did you ride that new horse that came in last week?"

"The palomino Arabian?"

"That's the one," she says, "The Western pleasure horse they want to try in endurance competitions."

"Yeah. He was in the trailer for six hours, so his owner wanted him to have a nice, easy leg-stretching ride the day he arrived, but she couldn't get out here." I come back around to the horse's near side. "Why? You have a thing for palominos?"

"He *is* pretty, but I'm asking you, because Becky asked me." She lifts her eyebrows.

"Oh. OK. Noted." Becky pays her salary, so Marge can't be caught talking about her behind her back, but she's just given me a clear warning that Becky's paying attention to the horses I ride – the ones she doesn't make any money on when I ride them. "Thanks."

I reach for the reins, but Marge holds onto them. "You get going. I'll look after him."

"But I rode him."

"Yes," she says. "And because of the way you rode him, I might have lined up a sale. He didn't even break a sweat – I just need to pull his tack off and put him back in his stall. Besides I assume you took the bus out here?"

I nod.

"Then go. It's nasty out there."

***

The snowflakes are so fat, I can hear them hitting the already-accumulated snow all around me. They make a soft *pat-pat-pat* sound. As much as I wish this deep snowfall hadn't forced me off my bike, I have to admit it's gorgeous.

The flakes just keep coming out of the black sky. Fast, like rain, landing with their steady *pat-pat*. Piling up on the sleeve of my jacket even as I watch.

They temper everything. The traffic noise from the big highway at the bottom of the driveway – reducing it to just a hum. The normally glaring beam from the nearby streetlamp – they flit in the cone of light it sends out, dancing like moths. The temperature – hovering just below zero despite the undeniable presence of winter, and the complete absence of the sun.

It's been a few minutes since a car's been by, and in that short time the snow has softened the outlines of the tire tracks.

A truck rolls up, creaking the fresh snow under its weight. The passenger window slides down. Inside, Drew leans into the snow-laced shaft of light. "What are you doing here?"

"Catching my ride home."

He laughs, but I'm not being funny. I point at the bus stop sign. "Should be here in fifteen minutes."

"You're not serious," he says.

I shrug. "You're right. It'll probably be closer to half-an-hour in this weather."

He's quiet for several seconds. "I can't offer you a ride home."

"Nope." I shake my head. "Rule of Two." There are still stables that resist implementing the Safe Sport practice that says no coach should be alone with an athlete. They say it's not practical in a sport that requires so much driving, and travel. But the rules are there for a reason, and when a stable has adopted them, I feel better about all their rider safety measures.

There's already a thin coating of snow on Drew's windshield. He bites his lip. The thought of leaving me here in the falling snow is obviously bothering him. "What if I did anyway?"

"I'd say no."

"Hmm ..." He snaps his fingers. "But I can give you money for a taxi."

"If you give me money, I'll ride the bus and put it in my show fund," I tell him.

He lets out a short, sharp laugh. "Don't you have parents?"

I nod. "I do. But they don't want me to ride. They say if I do, I'm on my own. And my parents stick to their word. Plus, they're on sabbatical in Peru."

Drew sighs. "Do you know my farm?"

What a question. It's like asking a basketball fan if she knows the Raptors. Well, nearly. "Yes."

"So, can you please do me a favour and email me when you get home this evening? The email address is on our website."

"Sure," I say it, but not like I mean it.

"No, I mean it," Drew says. "Give me your word and stick to it."

His windshield wipers give one big sweep, and he rolls forward before stopping and reversing again. "By the way, good assessment of that horse in there."

"I wasn't sure what to say—"

He cuts me off. "You did just fine. Diplomatic, but truthful." He winks. "I'm going to recommend the horse to my student. Watching you ride him showed me he has more scope than I thought he did. He'll give her room to improve without over-facing either of them."

"Right," I say. "Good. I'm glad. He's a nice horse. He deserves a good home."

"Speaking of which, you get along home now," Drew says, and this time he leaves for good.

***

I should try to read on the bus, but instead I replay the evening's events. Riding for Drew – even if it wasn't the world's best horse – I'm still going to count that as a milestone. Becky, though – there's something building there, between her stare-down, and Marge's careful warning. And Drew's question about my parents. Of course, that's not really what he was asking. He was really noting how strange my situation is. How different from other riders my age.

Although I'm aware of it often in the day-to-day details, I rarely step back and take a big-picture look at the reality that I'm a city-dwelling teenager with no independent means, and for some reason I've glommed onto the idea of making a living as a rider.

The people around me – Scilla, Dana, Marge, Mr. Wayne – each see parts of me and accept that's just who I am. Somebody willing to ride any horse, not have a social life, get to the barn under my own steam, try most kinds of workouts as cross-training. They're used to me and maybe they think it's a phase. It's just my thing. It will pass.

I don't think that's right, but maybe it is. Maybe that's what Drew sees with his fresh eyes and his years of experience training successful riders.

I keep telling myself that since I can't do things the way everybody else does, I'll just do them a different way – maybe Drew sees the futility in that.

The bus is cold, and the windows are fogged up. It's an uncomfortable ride. It would be nice to be going home to a busy house with people going about their evening activities. Maybe offering to make me a hot chocolate or a mint tea.

That's not my life, though. There are things I can change, but my strange family set-up, and my desire to make a living with horses are not those things.

I know what those things look like – I used to experience them with my Aunt Ginny. It's not that we were huggy, or mushy, but we did things for each other that showed our love. She would stay up much later than she wanted to, to give me late-night lessons after all the other barn work was done. I'd get up much earlier than I wanted to, to help her muck out the barn. We were a family.

Now she's gone, but I still hold the love of horses she instilled in me, and I don't need an alarm clock to get me up to run in the dark. Every time I snug my reflective vest in place and set off running with my breath puffing clouds in the frigid air, it's a tiny tribute to my aunt.

So, I guess it doesn't matter what Drew – or anybody – sees or thinks. I guess I'll keep going to the stables as long as there's a bus or a bike that will get me there.

***

When I get home, Gri-gri is delighted to see me, delighted to run around the backyard in the still-swirling snow, and delighted with the extra kibble I give him to make up for his dinner being late.

I make myself a mug of hot chocolate, submit some homework, then open my parents' latest update. They share one personal email address but take turns writing to me. I can tell which one is writing by what they write about. My mother specializes in artifacts, while my dad focuses on structures. Today's message goes into excruciating detail about a 4,000-year-old polychrome wall.

"It's from Dad," I tell Gri-gri.

The dog tilts his head and I say, "Yeah, I know, I don't know what polychrome is, either."

I sigh. They mean well. They're excited by their work, and they think I will be, too. I don't blame them for sharing. What I do blame them for is not being able to take a step back and realize horses to me are just as interesting as archaeology is to them.

I reply, sending a photo I took earlier of Gri-gri romping in the snow. I thank them for the housekeeping money they've e-transferred and ask if they can add a bit next time to cover the fees to join the cross-country ski team. I know they will. They understand cross-country skiing. They see it as a practical sport. I've tried to argue the role of horses in ancient civilizations as a reason for them to pay for me to ride, and they told me instead they'd be happy to pay for me to join them on a dig where I could help excavate ancient stables.

So, we remain at our impasse.

I'm about to close the laptop when I think of somebody who does understand my riding compulsion. I feel a little silly, as I send an email to drew@sto negates.xom. Thanks for letting me ride that horse for you tonight. I got home safely.

Chapter Ten

IT SNOWS EVERY DAY. My bike is now at the back of the shed, with the snow shovels in front of it and I have to accept it's probably going to stay that way until spring.

I catch a couple of lucky breaks. On the weekend, Dana has to drive her little sister to a birthday party at a wave pool not far from the barn. She drops me off on the way. Another day my next-door neighbour offers me a lift in exchange for me shoveling his driveway.

My good luck only lasts so long, though. Soon enough I'm back to public transit, nose down in a textbook – this time trying to make sense of the wave nature of light. I'm the only person on the bus, which is how I know the driver's talking to me when he says, "You're going to have to get out here."

I'm patient with him. Reasonable. I haven't seen him before. Maybe he doesn't know the route. "There's a stop about a kilometre up this road. At the end of the McKellar Stables driveway."

"The hill's too icy. The last driver couldn't get the bus up. They told us to cut out that part of the route until they can send a salt truck out." He shakes his head. "Sorry, but you'll have to walk." He says he's sorry but he's holding the door open for me. The wind swirls a gust of snow in. He really wants to move on.

"Right." I step out to find the road really is quite slick. Fine, then. I'll cut across the field. It's a shorter walk and there's no ice.

There's a lot of snow, though. Drifted thigh-deep in spots. I'm not even a quarter of the way to the barn at the top of the rise and my legs are wet – boots filled with snow.

A couple of ponies fall into stride with me. Their winter coats are so thick my hands leave lasting prints on their sides – like memory foam. Unlike me, they're toasty warm.

"Thanks, guys." I laugh, but mostly so I won't cry. I'm numb from the waist down. I think of how the wilderness is only ever so far away when you're in Canada. Even here where we're within the city limits of the nation's capital such that garbage gets collected from the curb and buses run. Some days. When the hill isn't too icy.

The sun's already dipped behind the big, bus-defying hill. The remaining light has a fuzzy, snowswirl-dimmed quality to it. It would be possible to get disoriented, wander around as full darkness falls, and die in the snow here.

Possible, but stupid. I'm not going to do it. I'm not even going to get frost-bite. I throw my arm over the nearest pony's neck and trudge on.

I'm in my (wet) sock feet in the bathroom, scooping snow out of my boots so it can melt in the sink, when the door swings open and Becky comes in.

Well, this is awkward for both of us.

Since we can't just ignore each other, I'm trying to think of a non-confrontational piece of small-talk I can use to get us through this moment, when her stance – squarely blocking the door – along with the narrowing of her eyes tell me she's not trying to ignore me, or to smooth over our encounter.

She came in here to confront me. She starts with, "I know what you're doing."

Really? Is she that petty? "My boots got full of snow. I'm just scooping it out. I'll wipe the counter when I'm done."

"Not that." Her voice is a hiss. "Stealing rides on horses."

How do you steal a ride on a horse? "I'm not stealing anything."

"Of course you are, and you know it. We charge for training rides. We lose money every time you ride somebody else's horse."

There's the tiniest pause – the most fleeting of moments – where I could try to end all this. Be conciliatory. Try to turn the tension down by a notch or two.

Instead of doing that, I give in to the pressure in my chest, and the tightness in my lungs, and say, "That's not stealing. That's outperforming you."

She flinches and it feels so good I continue. "It's not my fault people pick the service they like best."

Becky's cheeks rush red. "You won't get away with this."

I shrug. "Seems like you need to talk to your clients – not to me. Tell them they're only allowed to book training rides through you. If they agree, then you're good." It's easy for me to say, because I know the clients won't be happy.

Becky knows it, too. She doesn't have a good answer for me, but she does have a scary one. "You're just a snotty kid throwing your name around because your aunt rode for Canada once-upon-a-time. I hope you've enjoyed it, because it's over now."

That nearly does it for my self-control. The girl whose parents handed her an entire riding school is saying I'm privileged? I'm proud of my name, and I'm grateful for the knowledge that came with it, but when my aunt died, I didn't get her stable, or any money, or a horse. And I lost the one person who understood me completely ... the tears are rising but I'm not going to cry in front of Becky.

I lock my knees, clench my core, thrust my shoulders back, stand as straight as I can, and stare. Hold Becky's gaze. Don't back down.

It feels like ages, but is really just a few loaded seconds, before she says, "I mean it. You'll see," and leaves the room.

My knees give. Stomach heaves. Hands shake so hard I have to grip the edge of the counter to stop them.

I want to cry. Loudly. But these walls aren't soundproof and if I run into Becky again I don't want red-rimmed eyes to give me away, so I gulp, hard, and get Luna ready so I can ride her while the indoor arena is empty before the private lessons start.

Even though it's my least favourite thing, I work on leg yielding because I know it's good for the mare.

When I'm done, I clean her tack, even out her mane, and leave Scilla a detailed note.

Over-compensation is my way of reacting to adversity, and leaving the mare gleaming and her tack glowing goes a tiny way toward restoring my equilibrium. If this is the last time I ride here, nobody can say I left a mess behind me.

Drew's already teaching by the time I get back to the arena. I roll the door open just enough to slip in, climb into the bleachers, and zone into the rise and fall of his voice while I eat my sandwich.

It's easy to forget Becky while my brain is focused on drinking in everything Drew's saying to his student. Later though, when I have only my thoughts to accompany me on the walk to the bus stop ... *Forget it.* This girl is really having trouble with her left canter transitions.

"Hey!" It takes me a second to realize Drew's walking toward me. "Too busy eating your gourmet dinner to answer my question?" he asks.

I smile. "Sorry, I missed it."

"Did you notice their left canter transition?" He points back toward the girl and her horse now cooling out at the far end of the ring.

"I noticed they couldn't get it."

"Tell me your strategy for that. What would you do?"

I straighten on the bench. "I'd check the horse – from his shoes all the way through his legs and into his hips and back. Also, the fit of his bridle. Make sure he's getting the cues and that he's physically capable of doing the transition – not injured or sore. Then I'd tell her to go home and do pigeon pose."

"I told her to lift her left hip to let him swing through in the transition," Drew says.

I shrug. "Yes, correct, but what if she can't? What if her hip flexors are too tight? In this sport, we check the horse top-to-bottom. We wrap them, rub them, massage them. We tell the rider to make corrections in the saddle, but we rarely do unmounted work with them."

Drew narrows his eyes, and I suddenly realize I've been preaching at a guy with the highest coaching certification level in the country.

Who do I think I am? Maybe Becky's right that I'm a snotty kid. Maybe I just don't recognize it in myself. Maybe I've burned bridges here, at McKellar, and with Drew – two in one night.

"Come with me," Drew says and walks out of the arena into the barn.

I follow him, wondering if he's looking for a quiet spot to put me in my place so he doesn't humiliate me in front of everybody. He pauses at the barn door and I take a deep breath, roll my shoulders back and come up next to him.

I'm sorry. The words are on the tip of my tongue.

He points out at the snow-covered parking lot, and I don't know what I'm supposed to be looking at. "There, under the light." The only thing under the light is a silver pick-up, not old enough to be vintage, not new enough to tow a six-horse trailer and have heated seats. He holds out a set of keys. "I'd like you to drive that."

I wrinkle my forehead. "Where?"

He shrugs. "Wherever you need to. Home, tonight, so you don't have to take the bus, as a start."

"I can't take your truck."

He grins. "It's my son's truck."

"Well, I can't take your son's ..."

Drew turns around. "There you are. This is the girl I was telling you about – the one who's going to look after your truck for you."

I look up into a set of cheekbones I recognize. They still do that thing to me – send a flutter of butterflies beating through my insides. Making me feel the way I did after our varsity team won the cross-country city championships and Dana convinced me to go to a beach party to celebrate where somebody poured out hot chocolate spiked with Bailey's.

I'm smiling at him, and he's smiling back at me, and Drew's still talking. "This is my son, Darcey. He lives downtown for university. There's nowhere for him to park the truck. We'd like you to use it during the week – so you can ride and do whatever else you need. Then, on the weekend, you can pick him up and drive him home to us for a Sunday meal. It's a win-win."

I'm being offered exactly what I wanted – a quick and easy way to get to riding – just when I've quite possibly lost my chance to ride at all. Why is life like this?

I shouldn't accept the truck. It's too much for them to offer me. It's a big responsibility. If I have, indeed, been banned from this place, I'm taking it under false pretences.

But it feels so nice to have somebody want to take care of me. And it feels even nicer that that somebody has such a hot son.

"Well?" Drew's still dangling the keys. His eyebrows are lifted.

"There's something kind of important you haven't asked me," I say.

"Which is?"

"Whether I have a licence."

"Ha!" He throws his head back and laughs from his belly. "This one is funny," he tells his son.

"I know," Darcey says. "We've met."

"Right. Even better." He picks up my eye contact. "Do you have a licence?"

I nod, and it's answering more than just whether I'm a licensed driver. I take the keys. "Thank you."

"You come out, too," Drew says. "On Sunday. I have a couple of horses you can ride."

Chapter Eleven

THE WHOLE NEXT DAY I try not to think about Becky and the barn. I have a test in the morning and a lab in the afternoon, which helps keep my mind occupied. Then, after school, is the first cross-country ski team practice. We meet on the groomed path along the river.

Dana shows up, carrying skis that aren't hers. Dana doesn't much like the snow, or the cold. I raise my eyebrows. "What gives?"

Her eyes slide right past me to Pascal Oumarou. Tall, lean, funny, and kind. Fast, too. He led the boys' cross-country running team to the provincial finals.

Dana's had a crush on him forever.

"I didn't know he could ski," I say.

"He can do anything," Dana says.

"Including make you borrow your mom's skis and come out in the cold."

She nods. "Including that."

I resist the urge to give her a hard time. There's a truck parked in my driveway that I should have said no to, if a certain set of cheekbones hadn't persuaded me toward yes.

It's a beautiful afternoon – hard blue sky, bright (even if not very warm) sun. The shush-shush of skis over the sparkling white snow. Pascal leaving everybody else in a whirl of snowflakes. Dana skiing faster than I've ever seen her go before.

As I walk home with my skis slung over my shoulders, I think it was fun, but it's not riding.

The hollow feeling in the pit of my stomach has eased. The whole day's passed with no message from Becky. The only thing posted on the barn Facebook group today was a cartoon about a horse and a plastic bag, I'm starting to think – to hope – it's all blown over. Becky was mad, but she's calmed down now.

Maybe we can just go back to avoiding and ignoring each other. In retrospect, I have warm memories of that era.

I text Scilla – **You want me to ride Luna tomorrow?**

The answer comes quickly, **Of course.** She's probably wondering why I'd suddenly ask, but it's a test. To see if Becky's said anything to her.

The "yes" means everything's OK. I think. I pause in my driveway next to the truck and place my hand on the hood. The metal's cold now, and the truck's an older model, but the heating works, and it will get me warmly to the barn.

The temperature may be plummeting, but maybe everything will be OK.

***

Thanks to Drew's truck, I can wear my nice schooling clothes to the barn, including my new-to-me shiny tall boots, with no need to add layers and layers of waterproof and insulated outerwear. That inspires me to bring a length of sparkly Christmas ribbon to braid into Luna's tail. I'll try to get some nice photos I can share with Scilla for her to use in her holiday cards.

The barn's quiet when I arrive. It's too big to be homey, but it's familiar. My nerves ease as I walk through the aisles I've walked through hundreds of times before, open Luna's door giving the bolt the extra little jiggle it always needs, and open Scilla's locker to find two notes in the envelope there. Becky doesn't seem to be around and thanks to having the truck I'll have time to ride both those horses after I ride Luna.

"First, though, Operation Holiday Glow-Up," I tell the mare.

I'm humming to myself, looking through Scilla's locker for the red saddle pad that looks so festive, thinking how good Luna's going to look for my photos, when I hear the voice I'd almost forgotten about behind me.

"What do you think you're doing?"

It's Becky. So much for avoiding and ignoring.

"I'm tacking Luna up."

"You're not riding," she says.

The truth is, I'm not – at least not right now. I'm tacking her up for the photos. Still, I do plan to ride later, and I don't feel like backing down. Also, Scilla owns Luna, and Scilla wants me to ride her, so whatever Becky thinks about me riding other horses, I tell myself I have the right to ride this mare. I take a deep breath and say, "Yes, I am."

Becky scowls. "That's what you think." She hands me a letter. I take it automatically, and as soon as I do, she smiles. Not a nice smile. I liked the scowl much better.

I don't want to read this letter in front of her.

I want to read it even less when she folds her arms and tilts her head in a way that you could put in the dictionary to illustrate the word "smug."

But I do want to know what the letter says.

Hating myself for giving in to Becky, hating Becky for putting me in this position, I unfold the paper.

Be it known that as of the date inscribed above, you are hereby and forthwith banned from entering or conducting any manner of equine-related engagements, transactions, or otherwise horseplay within the sacred confines of McKellar Park Stables. This edict is issued under the auspices of our newly minted directive, which unequivocally prohibits the ingress and egress of outside contractors, freelancers, and other non-affiliated entities seeking to ply their trade upon these hallowed grounds.

Your flagrant disregard for the established decorum and the unilateral appropriation of our facilities for your personal gain has left us no recourse but to invoke this decree, ensuring the preservation of our esteemed stable's exclusivity and operational sanctity.

Let this missive serve as unassailable testament to our resolve. MPS is, has been, and shall remain private property, with rights of admission stringently reserved and enforced. Any attempt to contravene this prohibition will be met with the fullest extent of consternation and remedial action permissible by law and the ancient traditions of horsemanship that we hold dear.

Your compliance with this directive is anticipated posthaste.

My English teacher would give whoever wrote this a failing grade ... with a LOT of red pen. It has it all: passive language, pretentious wording, imprecise meaning. Although, I suppose one part of it is very clear, and it's the part that says I can't ride here anymore.

"You can't do this." I wonder if Becky can hear the breathlessness in my voice, or if it's just that I know all the air is gone from my lungs.

"I just did." I've never seen her give such a genuine smile – it's spread to her eyes.

"Just did what?" Scilla appears around the corner weighed down with a ten-pound bag of "naturally imperfect" (aka strangely shaped) carrots, and still another horse blanket I've never seen before. She was smiling – her own kind smile – but one look at my face and she repeats, "Did what, Becky? What have you done?"

Becky chooses not to answer, and I can't find the words. I swap the letter for Scilla's carrots, holding them awkwardly while she reads.

When she looks up, her eyes are narrow. She focuses them immediately on Becky. "I hope you've thought this through, young lady."

Becky's smugness is gone. Her face is flushed red. "I run this place now. I have the right to make decisions."

"Right then. Have you given a copy of this letter to Drew? And to Hilly Jensen? Or should I do that?" Scilla asks. "Come to think of it, it's probably easiest for me to just post it on the local forum."

"This has nothing to do with Drew, or Hilly, or anybody but *her*." Becky stabs her finger toward me.

"Did you not read it, Becky? The part about 'outside contractors, freelancers, and other non-affiliated entities seeking to ply their trade ...' That's Drew. And Hilly. And Performance Hoof Health – I know a couple of people who only decided to move their horses here once they heard Performance had agreed to be your new farrier."

I've heard people described as "open-mouthed," but the last time I actually saw someone with their mouth hanging open like Becky's is, was Jimmy Mackey in first grade ... and we found out later that he had adenoid problems and couldn't breathe through his nose.

Becky catches me staring and snaps her mouth shut. For a second her eyes narrow with anger, then uncertainty floods in. "It's not the same," she says.

If she was smart, she'd ask for the letter back, say it was a misunderstanding, and we could all try to forget this happened.

But that's not Becky.

Instead of asking, she snatches for the letter. "You have no right to do anything with that letter."

"You're right," Scilla says. "It's Laney's letter. She and I will discuss what to do with it."

Becky stands, clenching her jaw and her fists.

"Go on now, Becky, you've made your point and delivered your message," Scilla says. "It's time for you to give us some space."

Becky looks like she's about to protest that she delivered a note asking me to leave, and now she's the one being asked to go, but she looks at Luna and seems to remember, after all, Scilla is a paying customer and, with a kind of grunt, turns and leaves.

As soon as Becky pulls the barn door closed behind her, Scilla tells me, "Of course she's in the wrong. She's always been impulsive and too sure of her own opinion."

It's a nicer assessment than I would make of Becky.

"It's not over, Laney dear. You know I'm on your side, but unfortunately for the next short while, I'm afraid you should probably stay away. We'll put Luna away together then I'll give you a drive home."

My voice sounds strange when I answer. It's surreal that I can still speak when I've been cut off from the most important thing in my world. "It's OK," I say. "I have a truck."

"Goodness," Scilla says. "Since when?"

"Drew loaned it to me. So it would be easy for me to get out to ride." Something inside me crumples, compressing my lungs, making it hard to get the words out. Now that I have a truck to make riding easy, I don't have anywhere to ride. It makes all my complaining about taking the bus seem pathetic. At least I had a destination then.

Scilla's smiling though. "Ah, Drew." She pats me on the shoulder. "You see? You'll be just fine."

I don't feel fine, though. I drive home on autopilot. When I pull into the driveway, I can't remember any of the turns I took to get home.

Gri-gri is delighted to see me, but even his unconditional and pure delight in my presence can't fill the empty feeling inside me.

I do the only thing I've ever been able to do when I can't ride as much as I want to. The only thing that's delivered results when I can't get to the barn. I lace up my running shoes and go for my second run of the day, welcoming the numbness of the intense nighttime cold.

Chapter Twelve

I FEEL LIKE A zombie all the rest of the week. Not quite dead, but not sure what I'm living for.

True to her word, Scilla hasn't accepted the fight is over. The day after the confrontation she texts me to say she's having a meeting with Becky's parents.

I'm hoping they can help her see reason.

She may be hopeful, but as the numbness wears off, I'm not.

I stay behind after Fit for Life, working on my side planks. "Much better," Mr. Wayne says.

He's right … but for what? I can side plank, but I can't ride.

When I sniff, he asks, "Are you alright? Do you want to talk about it?"

His kind words almost undo me. I have to bite hard on my lip and stare over his shoulder before I can say, "Something's happened. I can't ride right now. I'm finding it very difficult."

I brace for him to say, "But there are so many other things you're good at. Focus on those." He's that kind of person – a glass-half-fuller.

Instead he says, "I'm sorry." Two words. Nothing concrete. But soothing – even if only temporarily.

I mean it when I say, "Thanks."

He continues. "My experience, for what it's worth, is that life is a series of chapters. Switching chapters can be hard."

I don't want this chapter to be over. The thought makes me angry, but not at him. "OK," I say. "I'll keep that in mind."

"Also," he says. "It never hurts to be able to side plank."

The next day Scilla texts. **Having a boarders' meeting at my house this evening. Will report back.** What I get from that is that the meeting with Becky's parents didn't help.

I send her a "Thank you," and a thumbs-up I don't feel.

Between classes I open an email from my parents saying the dig is at a crucial stage and they can't possibly leave, but they'll pay for me to fly to Peru for Christmas if I want to come.

"Peru ..." Dana reads over my shoulder. "*I* want to go!"

"I wish you could," I tell her.

She shakes her head. "If wishes were horses ..." then blinks. "Sorry."

"Nah," I say. "You're not wrong." If only my wishes were horses, but they're not.

I Google the cost of a flight to Peru, thinking it's enough to keep me riding for a couple of months. Except ...

The third day with no riding, Mr. Wayne finds me in the hallway at lunch. "I sent your cross-country times to a friend of mine who coaches track and cross-country at the university. He says he'll be at the provincial track meet this spring, and he won't be the only university coach there. I'm sure you can make a varsity team if you run track in the spring and we work together on your distance training."

Of course I love running. It keeps my head clear and it keeps me fit ... for the thing I really want to do, which is ride. It's never been my goal, though.

"Think about it," Mr. Wayne says. "Indoor track practices start the first week back after Christmas. There's a spot for you if you want it." He pauses, then adds, "It would be a different chapter."

"Thank you," I say. "I really appreciate it." He's right. It would be a new chapter. Except …

I could be on a university varsity team … *except*.

I could fly to Peru … *except*.

I have a truck … *except*.

I can side plank … *except*.

Maybe I'm just spoiled. Maybe I'm in denial. But the heart wants what it wants, and my heart doesn't want these things, no matter how great they might be.

Saturday brings a new text from Scilla.

> Luna and I miss you. The boarder meeting was helpful. People aren't happy with Becky. Some are threatening to leave. Next step is to talk to some of the other McKellar contractors.

> Thank you, Scilla. I appreciate it.

There's not much else I can say. I do appreciate Scilla's support, but I also know human nature. Talking about leaving, and actually leaving are two different things – especially when the barn's so close to the city. I can't expect that people will actually leave en masse when there's no other stable so easy to get to … which is ultimately my problem as well. Because I won't have Drew's truck forever, and if I'm banned from McKellar, there's nowhere else I can get to.

I know I have to stay busy, so I do all my homework, study for exams, which are still weeks off, and walk the dog more than he's ever been walked before. When the sun goes down, I take everything out of the fridge and scrub the inside, clearing out old condiments and sauces before putting the food back in. Well, that's something I've never done before – but at least it killed an hour.

All this time I walk by the truck several times a day and it's not lost on me that just when I finally have this vehicle to use for riding, I have nowhere to ride.

At least tomorrow I'll have something to do. I'll go pick up Darcey and I'll make arrangements to give the truck back. After all, it's not like there's any point in keeping it.

Chapter Thirteen

I SAID I'D DO this, so I'm doing it.

I'm a good driver, but all my driving experience has involved leaving the city. Heading onto wider roads, with more space.

It feels strange to turn off the highway ramp onto a busy main street lined with coffee and cannabis shops, and already narrowed by the early snow we've had – especially navigating it in this big pick-up truck.

Still, Drew and his family have been kind to me, so I'm not going to leave them in the lurch.

I slow and indicate to turn right, only to realize the street ahead is one way left.

This isn't going to work. I'm jangling with anxiety. It was nice of Drew to offer to let me ride a couple of horses, but he's well known for having his own ways of doing things – on his turf, there's every chance he won't like the way I ride. Plus, I'm essentially stepping into the middle of a family reunion – talk about a quick and easy way to feel like an intruder.

Then there's the biggie. I long to ride, and Drew said he has a horse for me to ride, but I'm afraid having that little taste will only make it harder to go back to my regular life, now with no horses in it.

I find a street where I'm allowed to turn right and mentally plan a route to get myself over to Darcey's building. Assuming I don't hit any more one-way streets ...

Maybe I should just hand Darcey the keys and ask him to drop me back at my house on his way home. I could even offer to take the train.

That would probably be best.

There's a familiar figure standing by the snowbank ahead. I pull over, and he opens the door and smiles. "Hi, you."

The bottom drops out of my stomach, my heart hammers in my chest, and I'm unable to say anything at all. Not even hello. Certainly not, *Can you just drop me off at home and go ahead yourself?*

Instead, I return his smile, and for the second time in the presence of this guy, I decide to pretend. Pretend I'm a normal girl in a truck with a guy I might conceivably date. Imagine I'm heading to ride with the best coach in the area, not as a fluke, but as a regular thing. What harm can it do to fantasize a bit?

"... Laney?" Darcey's voice reminds me to also visualize doing a good job of driving us both safely to the barn, which is exactly what I do as he tells me funny stories about his classes, and I laugh and keep my eyes on the road so I don't even have to glance sideways as we pass McKellar.

***

The first awkwardness hits me as I stand by the truck, turning the keys over and over in my pocket, watching as Darcey is engulfed in hugs from his mother and a younger sister. Because I used to show my aunt's horses, I've only been going to horse shows in this area for a couple of seasons, but I noticed these two early on. The mother is a beautifully quiet rider who makes every horse look their best, and the sister whips ponies around show-jumping courses fast and clean while making it seem easy.

"Hello, Laney!" Darcey's mother steps forward. "I always enjoy watching you show and I'm so glad Drew's finally persuaded you to come ride here. Mostly, though, thank you so much for bringing Darcey home for Sunday dinner."

I feel like clarifying that I'm riding a horse here today, as opposed to riding here – I hope she doesn't think I'm a well-off prospective new client. I'm also tempted to point out that I used their truck to bring Darcey here.

But she's being kind, and if the only time I'll ever see her again is from a distance at a horse show, it really doesn't matter, so I just smile and nod. "My pleasure."

Drew arrives from the barn. He gives Darcey a quick, fierce hug, then claps his hands and turns to me. "Come on now. I told you I have a horse for you to ride. Let's go!"

I try to keep up with Drew's long strides while also taking in the details of the barn we're walking through.

It's clean, orderly, and bright. Smaller than McKellar which makes it homier. A pony-tailed girl in riding clothes scoops wet shavings into a wheelbarrow in the aisle. I recognize her from Drew's show team. "How's Bibi's cut?" Drew asks her as we pass by.

"Improving!" she calls.

"Good," he says. "Your choice for tomorrow's lesson – you can ride him, and we'll take it easy, or you can use the new lesson horse if you want to jump."

He doesn't wait for her to answer. He's still moving, humming, snapping his fingers. Here, in his surroundings his energy is strong. The girl looks at me, shrugs, and smiles.

It's a good thing Drew's voice is loud because he's looking straight ahead, walking in front of me as he says. "You know Ji's horse, Bibimbap? They went to the provincial championships in the fall? Scraped himself on a sharp stick out in the field. Healing now."

"That's good." As nice a horse as he is, I'm not thinking about Bibi right now. There's a horse leaning out over a stall guard whose big, dark eyes, and striking face markings – a crooked white stripe snaking down to a fully white muzzle – take my breath away in the same way Darcey did when I first saw him. Except

I know what to think about horses, and I don't have to fake anything when it comes to this horse. I'm instantly in love and I'd be happy to admit it.

I've ridden some great horses over the years – horses I could never afford to ride if I was paying – but the downside of catching rides the way I do is that I don't get to choose.

I'd love to linger here, to take this horse out of his stall, and groom him, but Drew's still walking, and I need to see the horse he actually has in mind for me.

He stops in front of a stall containing a pretty dapple grey. "Seven-year-old mare," Drew says. "Sixteen hands. I'll show you where her tack is."

She's lovely, with great manners. Lifting her feet for me to pick them out. Standing quietly while I mount. Once I'm on her back she's forward, but not runny. Her strides are longer than I would expect from her size. She drops her head instantly to perpendicular with an arch in her neck – it's pretty but her frame's false. She's not really swinging through from her hind end. I work on transitions and a bit of collection to try to correct that.

At some point I become aware that Darcey's sister – Fee – is sitting in the corner. I have a real feeling of being watched, more than I usually do, even though generally somebody is always watching when I ride, even if just casually.

I can't figure out why, though. Drew sets up a few jumps and I think maybe now I'll find out what's up. Maybe the mare has a massive stop in her. Maybe she grabs the bit and plows through jumps. But no. She doesn't knock my socks off. I don't feel like she has limitless scope, but she's certainly capable of the mid-size jumps we put her over. She's well-mannered, responsive, picks up her feet.

It's a perfectly nice ride. Not that exciting, but with the mare's looks, definitely ribbon-worthy.

When I'm done, walking her on a big, long-reined circle, Drew asks, "What do you think?"

I think it's a trick question. I can't figure out the catch, though, so I just answer. "I think she's lovely. She's been well-schooled. She's very balanced – goey but doesn't run. In many ways she's a perfect horse." I'm telling the truth – she would be perfect for many people, even if my mind is jumping back to the white-muzzled horse I left behind in the barn.

"Ha!" Drew turns with his wide smile to Fee, who wrinkles her nose and nods. "Yeah, yeah ... point taken."

I'm completely confused. "What am I missing?"

"Dad bought her for me to show next year. Only problem is I can't get her over jumps. She runs out for me constantly. We've had the vet give her a once-over to see if there's something keeping her from jumping, but she has a clean bill of health. Dad said it's me ... and I guess now he's proven he's right since she jumped perfectly for you."

Awkward ... "I'm sorry." I wish Drew hadn't put me in this position.

"No," Fee shakes her head. "It's good to know. I really like her, and I thought we were going to have to sell her, but now I know she can do it, and I just have to work on it."

"Maybe Laney would have some ideas for you," Drew says.

"I'm sure Fee doesn't want my ideas." *I'm sure Fee would like to deck me right about now.* I probably would in her place.

It appears she's just as good-natured as her brother, though, because she gives me a smile that seems genuine and says, "I'd love to hear anything you have to say."

***

At first I'm not sure how long Fee and I have been in the arena when the door rolls open and reveals Darcey walking in. Then I notice how long and low the sun is and that the far end of the arena is mostly in darkness.

"Whoa," Fee says. "We've been here forever."

"No kidding," Darcey says. "Dinner's in half-an-hour. You'd better get a move on."

"OK, we will, but first you have to see what we've been working on! We've been having so much fun, haven't we, Laney?"

I nod. "We have." I really mean it. Having the whole arena to ourselves. Working with Fee and her horse with no time constraints. I forgot about my earlier anxiety. I forgot I was worried about fitting in here. Mostly I was able to completely forget my Becky-and-McKellar drama. I feel comfortable here in a way I never have at McKellar. If only Stonegate was located on a bus route and McKellar was out here. *If only wishes were horses …*

Fee's already out on the track, showing Darcey what we've accomplished with her pretty mare, Moonbeam. Moon's tack is off, the saddle placed on the arena boards, with the bridle lying across it.

I step back beside Darcey and we watch his sister walk along, her horse by her side. She stops and the mare does, too. She walks forward, turns into the centre, goes back to the track on the opposite rein, all with Moon keeping pace beside her.

"Watch this!" Fee giggles and breaks into a run. The grey mare trots beside her. Fee heads for a small X and Moon follows her over it.

They stop in the middle of the ring, with Fee pointing at Moon's hind end and the horse obediently cross-stepping away from her. First one direction, then the other. There's a smile on Fee's face the whole time.

"Nice work," Darcey says.

I shrug. "It really wasn't work at all – it was fun."

"Yeah, but that was kind of the point, wasn't it?"

He's right. As a serial catch rider I'm always trying to figure out how to get to know a horse quickly. Today I used some of my tricks to break down the tension I saw between Fee and her horse. *Fun* … In the fading light his eyes are dark. I look up to them and think, *I'd like to have fun with you* … He narrows his eyes and bites his lip, and while I'm busy not being able to tear my gaze away, he takes hold of my baby finger. Just the one finger. Just lightly. But it sends a fizz through me. I want him to hold my whole hand. Both of them. I want more.

"Hey. I thought we were running behind for dinner."

Darcey clears his throat, "Thanks for reminding me, Sis."

"My pleasure!" She loops Moon's reins around her neck, winks at me, and says, "You can carry her saddle for me, Darce."

I follow them both out of the ring trying to keep the wobble out of my knees.

Chapter Fourteen

I LEAVE FEE GROOMING Moon and carry her saddle and bridle into the tack room to clean them and put them away. Where the McKellar tack room is vast and sterile, this one is cozy, and doubles as a viewing lounge with a battered leather couch placed in front of a wide window gazing upon the arena.

Maybe I'll just chill here while the family has dinner. Oh, and go stare at the gorgeous monster bay who grabbed my attention earlier. I can think of worse ways to pass an evening.

It makes sense to keep this one space at a very comfortable twenty degrees, and also to have the plumbing clustered together. There's a powder room in the corner, and against its wall a double sink with a sign over one side declaring, **Horse Stuff** and the other side **People Stuff**.

I smile at the sign as I fill my tack-cleaning bucket, smile even more because the water's warm – it's something we didn't have at my aunt's farm, and I've been spoiled by having it at McKellar.

As I clean, I study an arrangement of photos displayed on the wall behind the tack hook. The older ones are in the centre. There's one looking up the long

Stonegate drive. Today the trees that line it are substantial, with many of their branches meeting overhead. In this photo, Drew and his wife stand at the end of the driveway with the trees on either side of them barely above their head height.

Another is of a much younger Drew flying over a massive cross-country jump on a muscular near-white horse. If I thought his coaching was impressive, this picture of him riding is remarkable.

The photos get newer as my eye follows them toward the edges of the wall. It's easiest to notice the years passing by watching Darcey grow from a roly-poly baby, to sitting on his first pony – getting taller, leaner, and more handsome as time goes on.

But ... I'm confused about the pictures of Fee. I thought she was younger than Darcey, but in some photos she looks older. I figure-eight Moon's bridle, carry it to the hook with her name on it, then step over to take a closer look at the photo wall.

"Just can't keep your eyes off the handsomest thing you've ever seen, can you?" Darcey grins as he walks into the room.

I point at the picture of his dad eventing. "You're right. What was the horse's name?"

"Ouch," Darcey says.

"You did ask for it."

He steps beside me and without me really knowing how it happened, he's taken my pinky finger in his hand again. I give him a sideways look. "That feels nice."

"I'm glad you think so."

For a few seconds we stand in silence. Our eyes are on the wall, but all my sensations are channeled through that baby finger.

Finally, I point with my free hand. "Your sister ..."

"Gemma."

"Excuse me?" I squint my eyes closed, then open them again. "I thought that was Fee."

He points to one photo. "That's Fee." Then a different one. "That's Gemma."

That explains my confusion about Fee and Darcey's relative ages. "Right. So Gemma is your older sister?"

"She was. She died."

His words rush ice through me. *Oh. No.* "I'm so sorry. I messed up."

He readjusts his grip to thread all his fingers through mine. "Of course you didn't. You never met her, and it happened so quickly that even people who knew her well were caught off guard. She had meningitis – we thought it was the flu – by the time we got her to the hospital the doctors tried, but they couldn't save her." He squeezes my hand. "The worst thing we could do is never talk about her. That's why my parents left all her pictures up here. In fact, Mom just found this one on her phone and got it framed. It's the last one we have of her riding."

I lost someone too. I think of telling him, but I'm afraid it might sound like I'm trying to make his loss about me. Instead I step even closer to the photo wall. "Is that ...?"

Darcey nods. "Yukon. The big bay with the stall guard. Gem only had him for a month or so before she died. Mom doesn't want to sell him. She tries to ride him, but I don't think she enjoys it ..."

We both turn to the door when Fee sticks her head in. "Hel-lo? Time? Dinner?"

"You need to thank Laney for cleaning your tack. You wouldn't be ready otherwise," Darcey says.

"Oh, I'm not questioning Laney ..."

I don't know these two well, but their banter makes me smile. Makes me wonder what it would be like to have a sibling of my own. Then again, they've also shared the pain of losing a sibling. Nobody's life is perfect.

I slide my fingers out of Darcey's, and he whips his attention back to me. "What are you doing?"

"You heard your sister. You need to get going for dinner."

"Oh no!" Fee says. "You are *so* not getting out of the full Hawthorne family meal experience."

Darcey tightens his fingers on mine just before I slip clear. "Is that what you were trying to do? No way. Fee's absolutely right on this one. We're counting on you to carry the conversation. The four of us are sick of each other."

Fee reaches for my free hand and gives me a tug, and apart from a quick glance back at the very handsome Yukon whom I never did get to meet properly, I'm quite happy to be escorted to the house.

Chapter Fifteen

THE TABLE IS ROUND so I don't have any sense of being a fifth wheel. Then, suddenly, I remember this table was meant for five people.

The energy of the family doesn't let me dwell on that, though. Fee bubbles with excitement describing the work we did with Moon.

"What gave you the idea to do that?" Darcey's mom, Andy, asks.

"My aunt taught me to ride. It was a thing at her barn. You couldn't get on your horse until you spent five minutes working with them on the ground first. And, after you got off, you had to spend another five minutes. Grooming time didn't count."

Andy nods. "Is your aunt's barn nearby?"

"It was near North Bay. I used to spend all summer and every holiday there." I take a deep breath. "Unfortunately, she died, and the farm was sold. That's why I've been catching rides here the last year or so."

"I'm sorry for your loss."

"Thank you," I say. "It was hard, but I'm getting used to the way things are now."

"That's a good way of putting it," Andy says. "You get used to the way things are."

"I'm sorry for you, too." I don't know if it's the right thing to say, but sitting here in what was probably her daughter's chair, I don't feel like I can avoid it.

"I could get used to Darcey not putting half a bottle of ketchup on everything he eats," Fee says.

"I could get used to you minding your own business," he replies.

And they're off in a volley of good-natured back-and-forth. I like sitting back, listening, feeling part of something but not having to make any effort.

It's true I'm self-sufficient, and I don't mind eating dinner with Gri-gri and a good book for company … but this is nice for a change.

The conversation flows into everybody's schedule for the week. Fee, like me, is in her last year of high school. "English essay, yearbook club meeting, groundwork with Moon!" She shoots me a sideways grin.

Darcey groans. "It's all about studying for exams … which you could argue I should be doing now."

His mom reaches out and taps his hand. "You need to eat. And interact with other human beings. This is good for you." Under the table he bumps his foot against mine and I'm glad he's interacting with me.

Andy says, "Believe it or not, I'm in full show-planning mode. I have calls lined up with a few potential sponsors, which is promising."

Drew grins. "Mine's easy. Horses."

God, I wish. I hope they don't ask me about mine, because it would be easy, too. *No horses.*

He continues. "Although, there is one other thing …"

He looks around the table and the rest of them nod. I have that feeling again, like I did earlier in the arena after riding Moon. Like there's something I'm not quite getting.

"It's about you, Laney."

My heart is doing a weird pump-flutter. *Have I done something wrong?* I rack my brain.

Drew glances at Andy and she takes over. "Darcey said he told you about Gemma." She pauses and I nod. "As you and I just discussed, it takes a while to get used to somebody being gone. Quite early on, our family knew we wanted to do something that would be a legacy for her, but it was only recently that we figured the best thing would be a kind of scholarship to help a promising young rider."

She nods at Drew – *over to you* – and he says, "We'd like that rider to be you."

My body takes an involuntary inhale, then freezes. I automatically cover my mouth with my hand. Buying time? Signifying I'm not ready to talk? I don't know – it's not conscious. It just happens. I force myself to lower my hand and speak. "I'm not sure …"

"Right," Drew says. "Well, we aren't either. Or we weren't. What form would a scholarship take? Would the person have to ride here? Would it be a lump sum? We just didn't know."

Andy smiles. "Then Drew came home, talking about this girl he met. Telling me she was different than any of the riders we know – that she rides the bus to get to the barn. That she'll ride any horse she's put on. He told me he thought she – you – could ride Yukon, and that was the clincher."

"Yukon?" I think of the big, handsome horse. I'd give a lot to climb on his back.

"So will you?" Fee asks.

"You know about this too?"

Darcey speaks up. "We all had to agree. We all do agree." He smiles. "But you might be wondering about the details."

Drew takes over again. "It might evolve but, essentially, we'd like you to join our community. To treat Yukon like your horse. To have lessons with me once or twice a week. To show with our show team. You'd use the truck like you did today. If you want to, of course."

I want to! I want to scream it out, but …

"Shouldn't I have to pass some kind of screening?"

Drew belts out that hearty laugh of his. "What do you think the last few weeks have been, kiddo?" Then, more seriously, he says, "We all know what

Gemma was like. We get to pick the Gemma Hawthorne Scholarship recipient. We think it should be you."

I'm clasping my own hands together tightly under the table. I want this so badly.

"I should talk to Scilla – Luna's owner from McKellar? She's been helping me."

"By all means, talk to her," Drew says. "But I think you'll find she already knows."

I remember her last text message – that she was going to contact some of the other contractors. I remember her comment about me having Drew's truck. It all makes sense.

I take one short moment to consider what would happen if Scilla told me she sorted it all out, and I could go back to McKellar? I look at each of the faces around the table. The warm kitchen cluttered with cooking pots. I think of the friendly, well-run barn, and I think of Yukon's big head, leaning out into the aisle – waiting for me.

Then I think of Mr. Wayne's words. This is my new chapter.

"I'd like to accept," I say. Then I shake my head. "Actually, I'd *love* to accept."

***

We left Fee and Drew washing dishes. Andy working on her laptop – "I'm so excited! I'm adding you and Yukon to all our show lists." Darcey had been tasked with taking me out to the barn to meet my new show horse.

He's even more gorgeous close-up. He's more gorgeous now that he's – sort of – mine. I admire the chrome splashing up his legs, matching the bright white of his nose. I scratch behind his ears and instantly hit on a spot that makes him stretch his head out and flap his lips. I stand quietly while he snuffles all over my face and hair.

"Get to know me," I whisper, "because we'll be hanging out for a while."

Darcey doesn't interfere. He doesn't remind me to hurry it up because I'm his ride back to the city and exam-studying awaits. He lets me and the big horse get to know each other then he reaches out and straightens Yukon's forelock and says, "I'm glad he has a person now ... and I'm glad that person is you."

It only seems right to stand on my tip toes and, with one hand twined through Yukon's mane, run my other hand into Darcey's thick hair and pull his lips to mine.

They're soft and warm and I can feel the kiss straight through the centre of my body. *Oh, my, wow.*

"So," I ask. "Does this mean there's no prohibition on a member of the family kissing the Gemma Hawthorne Scholarship recipient?"

"Not as long as the recipient is you." Then he leans in and kisses me back to prove his point.

THE END

***

If you liked this book ...

... you might enjoy Tudor's other books. Read the first chapter of Objects in Mirror, Book One in the Stonegate series, to find out.

Chapter One — Objects in Mirror

The whipper-in calls my number – "Seventy-two, you're on deck!" – and, as though he understands that's us, Sprite dances sideways, nearly slamming the clipboard-wielding gentleman into the white fence boards.

This is the big class of the day. I'm as excited as Sprite, but one of us has to stay calm. Serenity doesn't come naturally to hepped-up off-the-track thoroughbreds like Sprite. Which leaves me to be the sensible one.

I sink my heels deeper in my stirrups, settle my seat more firmly into the saddle, and point my thumbs up.

Back straight, big smile, look cool, and send Sprite, in his beautiful sweeping trot, into the ring.

Where he promptly grabs the bit, yanks his head down, and lets his back heels fly.

Sprite wants to jump. Sprite sees no need to bend or flex; to circle or warm up. He enters the ring with his eyes and ears flicking from jump to jump.

In Sprite's mind, all I'm good for is pointing him at the first obstacle, after which I should back off and stop bugging him so he can finish the course.

I've ridden horses that can autopilot courses. Some of my competitors own horses like that. Sprite, however, is not one of those horses. Given his head, Sprite would jump everything twice, then get bored and jump the fence out of the ring, to keep on running and jumping everything in his path.

I know this because I've seen him do it.

So I give him a firm half-halt as I smile wider than ever, mutter "bugger" under my breath, and step him into the forward canter we need for our approach to the first fence.

He clears it by eighteen inches, and jump two, as well. He leaves at least two feet between his belly and the top rail of jump three and throws in a tail flourish on the landing. *Here we go.*

Sure enough, as he rounds the far corner, Sprite throws out a lightning-fast series of bucks. There are always three in quick succession, and those trademark three bucks will leave me only four or five precious strides to set him up for the diagonal combination.

"Excuse me!" I use my seat and my legs and my hands and my voice, too – a horse like Sprite requires every aid in the box – and we battle our way over the three increasingly wide jumps. By the end of the line, he's flying, reaching, digging, and the sturdy white ring fence is coming faster and faster, and we need to turn the corner in enough control to get over the tall vertical propped on the short end.

"Listen!" I tell him, but it's a tool for me too, reminding me first and foremost to get it done. Forget pretty, forget elegant; those can come later if we make the flat phase but for now, my priorities are (1) don't knock down any jumps, (2) don't die.

We dig in deep to the base of the vertical and, with a super-athletic effort, Sprite twists himself over it without bringing the rail down. To celebrate, he indulges in his biggest buck yet.

Despite all the noise and activity of the show grounds, all I can hear is my own voice ordering Sprite to "Smarten up!" then Drew's yelling, "Go, girl!"

"Go!" I tell Sprite. *Go, go, go*, and, with that, we're not fighting any more. We're four jumps from being home and we want the same thing – to get over them fast and clean – I lean forward, give Sprite a nudge, and soften my hands.

The new gear he clicks into is so fast it's almost scary. I hardly have time to breathe, as Sprite pins his ears against his neck, throws all his energy forward, and jumps the jumps.

When he's not in mid-air, he's running flat-out, and when he clears the last jump, I have to keep him galloping around the ring because there's no way I can stop him in time for a polite exit from the gate.

Fantastic, amazing, exhilarating, unbelievable. I'm hooked, hooked, hooked. Want to go right back in and do it again. Want to jump like that all summer long.

"Pinch me!" I tell Drew as I ride out of the ring, because I can't believe Sprite's mine for the season and I *do* get to do this all summer long.

"Don't relax yet," Drew tells me. "You're through to the flat. Now you've got to make him behave."

***

Four days later, my Sprite-induced jumping high hasn't worn off. It doesn't hurt that we placed third; an amazing showing, considering Sprite had to suffer through the flat portion of the class.

It's not like school's been distracting me. With the temperature hitting twenty-eight by fourth period, even the teachers are more focused on beaches and cottages than learning objectives and curriculum.

When I get on the school bus for my final ride of the year, and settle my butt onto the ripped vinyl of my usual seat, I have nothing left to think about – nothing to plan for, study for, or worry about – other than riding, and showing, and Sprite. I drift into a play-by-play rerun of our weekend jumping round so vivid that half my brain's still back at the show grounds as I step off the bus at the end of our gravel country driveway.

Only to be rugby-tackled around the knees.

"Ooof!" I yell. My arms flail for something, anything, to break my fall. Finding nothing, I go down hard, hitting the ground with a thump, swiftly followed by the second thump of my backpack full of books, bouncing off the gravel to hit me on the head.

"I'm Sowwy, Gwacie!" It's Jamie, my three-year-old brother, straddling my waist.

"I might believe you if you didn't look so happy," I tell him.

"Come on, you; give Grace some peace." Annabelle says, hauling him off, then holding out her hand to help me up. "He's so excited to see you. He can't stop talking about how you're going to be around all summer long."

Jamie runs off ahead of us, weaving from side to side across the driveway, stopping every now and then to make a wild jump in the air or kick out at his shadow. He reminds me of Sprite but without the bad nature.

"He insisted we make lemonade for you." Annabelle's trying, just that little bit too hard, to keep her voice light and easy. How can one simple sentence be so loaded, mean so much more than the sum of its words?

"Good," I say. "I'm hot." And Annabelle smiles. I've said the right thing: *I'll have some,* just not in so many words.

She takes my hand and, even though I'm nearly sixteen and, even though she's my stepmom, I let her. Even squeeze back a bit and, actually, it feels quite nice.

To continue reading Objects in Mirror, *use this QR code to get your copy now!*

Please leave a review!

Reviews help me sell books. More sales let me write more books. A simple star rating and a few quick words are all it takes to help other readers decide if they want to read my books.

Please write a short review of this book, at the retailer where you purchased it using this link: https://books2read.com/catchrider, or this QR code:

or review on Goodreads: https://www.goodreads.com/book/show/210086004

To make sure you don't miss my next release, sign up for my newsletter at this link: **www.tudorrobins.com/contact**, or use this QR code:

Other Books

Island Series:

Six-Month Horse (Prequel)

Appaloosa Summer (Book One)

Wednesday Riders (Book Two)

Join Up (Book Three)

Faults (Book Four)

Reason Why (Book Five)

Stonegate Series:

Catch Rider (Prequel)

Objects in Mirror (Book One)

After Lucas (Book Two)

Throw Your Heart Over (Book Three)

Perryside Series:

Moving North (Book One)

Mystery Stables:

Stolen Saddles (Book One)

Horse Books for Grown-ups (18+):

Before & After (Women's Fiction)

Not so Bad (Women's Fiction)

In Search Of (Small-Town Romance)

About the Author

Tudor Robins is the author of books that move. She wants to move your heart, mind, and pulse with her writing.

A little piece of Tudor's own heart is in many places: the central-Ottawa neighborhood where she grew up and still lives, the Gatineau hills and Eastern Ontario countryside where she loves to hike, Wolfe Island and the St. Lawrence River where she loves swimming and paddleboarding, and the university towns that are currently home to her children.

When she's not writing, Tudor loves riding, running, quilting, and walking and talking with her best friends and her Jack Russell / Potcake mix, Cara.

Tudor would love to hear from you at tudorrobins@gmail.com.